VIRTUAL CRIME,
REAL PUNISHMENT.

TOM CLANCY'S NET FORCE™

*Don't miss any of these exciting adventures
starring the teens of the Net Force ...*

VIRTUAL VANDALS

The Net Force Explorers go head-to-head with a group of
teenage pranksters on-line—and find out firsthand that virtual bullets can kill you!

THE DEADLIEST GAME

The virtual Dominion of Sarxos is the most popular war-
game on the Net. But someone is taking the game too seriously ...

ONE IS THE LONELIEST NUMBER

The Net Force Explorers have exiled Roddy—who sabo-
taged one program too many. But Roddy's created a new
"playroom" to blow them away ...

THE ULTIMATE ESCAPE

Net Force Explorer pilot Julio Cortez and his family are
being held hostage. And if the proper authorities refuse to
help, it'll be the Net Force Explorers to the rescue!

THE GREAT RACE

A virtual space race against teams from other countries will be a blast for the Net Force Explorers. But someone will go to any extreme to sabotage the race—even murder . . .

END GAME

An exclusive resort is suffering net thefts, and Net Force Explorer Megan O'Malley is ready to take the thief down. But the criminal has a plan—to put her out of commission—*permanently* . . .

CYBERSPY

A "wearable computer" permits a mysterious hacker access to a person's most private thoughts. It's up to Net Force Explorer David Gray to convince his friends of the danger—before secrets are revealed to unknown spies . . .

SHADOW OF HONOR

Was Net Force Explorer Andy Moore's deceased father a South African war hero or the perpetrator of a massacre? Andy's search for the truth puts every one of his fellow students at risk . . .

TOM CLANCY'S
NET FORCE™

PRIVATE LIVES

CREATED BY

Tom Clancy and **Steve Pieczenik**

BERKLEY JAM BOOKS, NEW YORK

TOM CLANCY'S NET FORCE: PRIVATE LIVES

A Berkley Jam Book / published by arrangement with
Netco Partners

PRINTING HISTORY
Berkley Jam edition / March 2000

The Penguin Putnam Inc. World Wide Web site address is
http://www.penguinputnam.com

ISBN: 0-425-17367-4

BERKLEY JAM BOOKS®
Berkley Jam Books are published by The Berkley Publishing Group,
a division of Penguin Putnam Inc.,
375 Hudson Street, New York, New York 10014.
BERKLEY JAM and its logo
are trademarks belonging to Penguin Putnam Inc.

PRINTED IN THE UNITED STATES OF AMERICA

10 9 8 7 6 5 4 3 2 1

We'd like to thank the following people, without whom this book would not have been possible: Bill McCay, for help in rounding out the manuscript; Martin H. Greenberg, Larry Segriff, Denise Little, and John Helfers at Tekno Books; Mitchell Rubenstein and Laurie Silvers at BIG Entertainment; Tom Colgan of Penguin Putnam Inc.; Robert Youdelman, Esquire; and Tom Mallon, Esquire; and Robert Gottlieb of the William Morris Agency, agent and friend. We much appreciated the help.

1

"Everybody else is here," Megan O'Malley told Matt Hunter as she met him at the door to her house. Her hazel eyes blazed as if she were accusing him. "You're almost late."

"Um—sorry." Matt blinked, then thought for a second. "Hey! Isn't *on time* good enough these days? Are you trying to make me feel guilty?"

"You're right. It's my turn to say 'sorry.'" Megan looked a little stressed out despite her smile. "I didn't mean to snap at you. It's just that I've got a three-ring circus running in the living room. How do you guys manage things when David has you over?"

"David never has more than four people over at a time," Matt said. "With his kid brothers on the rampage, that's about as many people as his folks' apartment will hold."

He glanced at the plate of assorted snacks in Megan's hand. Come to think of it, he was a bit hungry. . . . "And his idea of entertaining people is to turn the holovision on. He doesn't generally provide food."

"Speaking of holovision, that's what we'd better do," Megan said, looking at her watch. "The show should be on any minute."

The show was *Washington Personalities,* a long-running and highly regarded local news show where reporters interviewed some of the interesting but less-well-known folks who lived and worked in the capital. The reason Megan had invited everyone over was today's guest. Captain James Winters was going to be featured on this broadcast.

Captain Winters was a Net Force agent, a member of the special bureau of the FBI responsible for policing the web-work of computers that strung together the country and, indeed, the world. Besides being a crack federal agent, he was also the liaison for the Net Force Explorers.

Matt was a Net Force Explorer. So was Megan, and so were all the other kids sitting expectantly in her living room. Matt, Megan, Catie Murray, Andy Moore, Maj Green, P. J. Farris, David Gray—most of them had met at Net Force Explorers meetings. They'd become friends through the experiences they'd shared.

The Net Force Explorers had proved to be much more than a high-profile computer club for all of them. The kids had learned a lot about technology—and each other—while taking part in some pretty wild adventures.

And the man who'd always been there for them, even when they sometimes went off the deep end, was Captain Winters. All the kids were pleased that he was getting his fifteen minutes of fame.

Andy waved Matt over to where he sat on the couch, pointing to a lumpy object down by his feet. The wise-guy grin on Andy's face was as typical of him as the disheveled state of his blond hair. "Last one in gets the weirdest seat," he announced.

"It's not weird," Megan protested. "It's retro."

Andy gave her a look. "Which means?"

"It's a phrase from back in the 1990s. That's when this antique beanbag chair was probably made—unless it dates back to the 1960s."

"Oh," Andy said sarcastically. "So *retro* means 'old junk.' " He grinned at Matt. "Enjoy your seat."

"You can enjoy it, too," Megan told Andy. "You got in

just ahead of Matt—and stole my seat on the couch when I went to let him in."

Andy put on a big act of looking hurt. "You're the hostess—I thought you'd want me to have this seat."

"I might have, if you hadn't gone making fun of my beanbag chair." Megan handed the tray of snacks to Catie, grabbed Andy by the arm, pulled him off the sofa, and plopped down in his place.

"You can join me down here," Matt said, sinking into the beanbag. "It's surprisingly comfortable."

"Probably give me mildew," Andy groused, flopping down. He glanced up at Megan. "She sure is feisty," he muttered. "Think that's what keeps Leif interested in her?"

"I didn't even know he was," Matt said, glancing at Andy in surprise. Leif Anderson was another of the Net Force Explorers, but he lived in New York City most of the time. Even though his dad had tons of money, Leif wasn't able to come flying down to Washington, D.C., on a school day.

"Hey, is somebody recording this for Leif?" Matt asked.

"Already taken care of," Megan assured him. "So cut the sound—the show's starting."

The HoloNews logo swam into existence over the projection unit from Megan's family computer. Tinny, canned theme music began to play as cheesy computer graphics formed the letters *Washington Personalities*.

Matt shrugged. Well, after all, this was no prime-time show with a big budget.

A young news announcer grinned from the holographic projection. "It's Thursday, September 18, 2025, and this is *Washington Personalities*. I'm your host, Jay-Jay Mc-Guffin, and my guest represents a well-known law-enforcement agency—with a surprisingly human face."

The camera pulled back to show McGuffin sitting in an armchair that looked like an overgrown, hollowed-out billiard ball. Seated across from him, looking uncomfortable in a similar chair, was Captain Winters.

"Jay-Jay is right," Andy kidded from the peanut gallery. "Winters *does* have a surprisingly human face. And would you call those things they're sitting on retro chairs?"

"Shhhh!" Megan swatted him on the head. Matt always found himself a little in awe of the captain. Even in a sport coat and open-necked shirt, there was something undefinably military about the man. He made the casual clothes look like a uniform. But he smiled, looking definitely human as he responded, "Thanks, Jay-Jay. It's a pleasure to be here."

Jay-Jay McGuffin ran through a quick series of questions to establish exactly who James Winters was. Then he threw in a curveball. "You went from being a colonel in the Marines to being a captain in Net Force. Does that rate as a demotion?"

"Well, not in terms of pay," Winters replied with a quick grin. "And, as a Marine, I was responsible for keeping almost a thousand young men combat-ready—and for keeping as many of them as possible alive if we actually got into a fight. While it is in many ways equally—maybe even more—important work, apprehending computer criminals for Net Force is not, thankfully, such a life-and-death business." He paused for a second. "Especially when you consider my major assignment."

Matt was impressed by the way Winters fielded the question. But then, handling the media must be part of his liaison duties. Certainly, he had just managed to steer the interview in the direction he wanted.

"That's right," McGuffin said, "you're the national coordinator for the Net Force Explorers. Why don't you tell us a little about the group?"

Winters had a lot to tell, and as far as Matt was concerned, the captain did it very, very well. Jay-Jay McGuffin, however, was less impressed. "Is it appropriate to use a youth organization to recruit for a government agency?" the newsman asked.

"Man, he's really getting on the captain's case," Andy complained. "If any of us gave Winters that much grief, he'd let us know about it."

Winters's years as a Marine had given him lots of experience in how to cut someone down to size with a single glance or a few well-chosen words. Matt had been on the receiving end of that skill a few times. Andy and Leif had gotten more than their share of the captain's technique.

The captain sounded downright pleasant as he explained that the Net Force Explorers operated as a social and educational organization. "The kids are strictly civilians. We don't give them police training, and they have no police powers."

As the captain spoke, Matt wondered if Winters was thinking about the kids in this room and some of the cases they'd gotten involved in. As the man said, Net Force Explorers had no police powers. But that hadn't stopped Matt and his friends from testing their nerve—and their computer smarts—against spies, criminals, and terrorists.

"To give my personal opinion, I'd be proud to serve beside any of the young people in the Net Force Explorers," Winters finished. "They are a fine bunch of people, and I'm very proud of them. But they all have their own lives to lead. I'd never dream of trying to influence their choice of careers."

"Maybe Net Force *is* for me," Andy said.

"Dream?" Megan snorted. "Make that the captain's nightmare."

A car ad came on, and Megan got up to go to the kitchen and get sodas. Matt went to help.

"It's nice to see the captain get a little credit for the job he's doing," Matt said as he picked up a tray full of glasses. He grinned. "I bet we could make a nice profit out of bootlegging copies of this holo."

Megan shrugged. "If kids are that hot to see it, they can probably log on to the local HoloNet site."

"It might be a good idea to get the word out. If there's a big response, the show's producers will know they did a good job."

"I just wish it didn't have to be so phony," Megan complained. "Like that supposedly tough question that Jay-Jay guy asked." She rolled her eyes. "As if anybody named Jay-Jay could act tough!"

"David always makes fun of that," Matt said.

"I mean, do reporters think we're stupid?" Megan thumped more glasses down on another tray. "Do they believe we can't see through this act they put on, their eternal, life-and-death struggle for the truth . . . on a puff-piece interview show?"

"I guess it sells advertising," Matt said.

"And advertising gives the people who watch a chance to go to the bathroom." Megan picked up her tray. "Or to go and get a snack."

They returned to the living room and passed out the drinks. By the time they'd settled down, the show was back on. Captain Winters played some recorded holograms of local Net Force Explorers in action.

"Hey!" P. J. Farris pointed. "That's the exhibit we took around to all the senior centers, teaching about Net fraud and the elderly."

Hoots burst out in the room. "Is that some old lady's dog?" Catie crowed.

"No, it's Moore's hair!" Maj giggled.

Andy ran a defensive hand through his unruly thatch. "Nobody said they were recording that!" he complained. "That isn't fair!"

David chuckled. "Welcome to the wonderful world of broadcast news."

The segment was obviously coming to an end. Jay-Jay McGuffin shook hands with Winters. "Thanks, Captain. You give a very professional interview."

Winters responded to the back-handed compliment with a quiet "Thank you."

But the newsman didn't offer a jolly farewell. Instead, he gave his guest a smile with an undertone that Matt found unpleasantly sly.

"I wonder, though," Jay-Jay continued, "if you'd have been so cool and collected if you'd come in here knowing that Stefano 'Steve the Bull' Alcista was being paroled today? Isn't he the organized-crime figure who was accused of conspiracy and murder in the car-bombing that killed your wife?"

For once, James Winters didn't have an answer ready. He sat in shocked silence.

But Megan's living room was anything but quiet.

"Did he say what I thought he said?" P. J. demanded at the top of his voice.

"What kind of cheap crap—" David stormed.

"I never even heard that Captain Winters *had* a wife," Megan said.

Matt had never heard such a thing, either. But he was more struck by something he'd never *seen* before. On the holographic projection, caught in tight close-up, the still-silent James Winters fought to control his emotions and turn his face into an impassive mask.

But he was failing.

Matt couldn't turn his eyes way. It was like watching the aftermath of a mammoth car wreck—horrible, but mesmerizing.

There was the face he'd seen at dozens of Net Force Explorers meetings, but now, for the first time ever, Matt saw it distorted by fierce, deadly—and possibly even murderous—fury.

2

Megan surged to her feet and snapped a command at her family's computer suite. The holographic image of Captain Winters's angry face disappeared like a popping soap bubble.

I thought she was recording this for Leif, Matt thought. But now was obviously not the time to bring that up.

"We don't need to see any more of *that,*" Megan said angrily. "Or any more of that newsman's smirking face."

"I'm gonna call up HoloNews right now and see if I can get his butt fired." Maj Green's voice was too loud and her face was red.

Rummaging through her bag, she came out with her wallet. Maj flipped through IDs, transit passes, and credit cards until she came to a shiny silver surface. This was the foil-pack keypad, a control center built right into the wallet. Hidden circuitry imbedded in the heavy plastic could be instructed to run in various modes.

Maj punched in the code to turn the wallet into a phone with short, emphatic gestures. Her fingers tapped through another code, and she glared at a readout.

"The station's number is 555-1100," she announced, extending her glare to everybody in the room. "What's the problem? Am I moving too fast for you all? Where are those phones, people? We've got a career to fry!"

"I don't know if I want to go *that* far," David Gray said slowly, digging out his wallet. "But the question was cruel—and crude. We don't need that kind of attack journalism. That's what I'll tell them."

"These news-idiots don't think. They just go for the hottest buttons to push," Andy complained. Like David, he pulled out his wallet and began dialing.

"News-idiots is right," Catie fumed. "Mass-media reporters have been at this for—what? Eighty years now? And they still ask the stupidest questions. I did a report on the early space missions. The clips of the flights I studied were amazing. You'd see these clowns shove a microphone in the face of some astronaut's wife to ask, 'How will you feel if the rocket crashes?' Well, duh! What a surprise when the poor woman starts crying her eyes out!"

She came up with her wallet.

"What's that number again?" she asked.

In moments, all the Net Force Explorers were in phone mode, calling the local broadcast station with various messages in mind. They mostly got busy signals.

"We're probably overloading the local node," Megan said with a sigh, cutting off her call.

"Maybe some of us should hold off and see if the others have more of a chance," Matt suggested.

"Let the people who are really hot on talking to the station go first," David said with a glance at Maj. "A couple of us could call round to other Net Force Explorers. Let's see if we can't get calls coming in from all over the city."

Maj and Andy chose to keep pounding on the HoloNews switchboard. David switched his wallet circuitry to directory mode and began calling out phone numbers. Matt and Megan dialed those numbers in, calling on other Net Force Explorers and asking them to spread the word.

By the time Matt headed for home, the kids had created a new, growing—and very angry—grass-roots movement. Still, as he went to turn on the evening news, Matt hoped he wouldn't see a story on the release of Stefano "The Bull." It wasn't that he expected to see James Winters's disturbing reaction again if the reports were on the news. Or that he wanted to avoid looking at it, either. But he figured images of the *capo* getting out of jail would upset the captain. Matt hoped Captain Winters could be spared that pain.

Luckily, the usual turbulent politics of the Balkan Peninsula came to the rescue. NATO air power was moving against terrorist safe havens inside the Carpathian Alliance after a particularly ugly bomb blast in a market town across the border. The newscast was full of military briefings, hollering in the U.N., and street demonstrations. For tonight, at least, the attention of HoloNews—and its viewers—was focused thousands of miles away from a local organized crime boss strolling to freedom. *Thank God,* Matt thought, watching the sports come on.

Leif Anderson winced as he popped into virtual reality. *Time for another adjustment to the lasers on my computer-link couch,* he thought, riding through the pain and mental static.

Like almost everyone above the age of five, Leif had special circuitry implanted around his skull so he could directly interface with computers. But an attack by some cyber-vandals who'd committed mayhem at a baseball game Leif had attended had increased his neural sensitivity to veeyar transmission—almost, though not quite, to the point of rendering it impossible. Unless every component of the process—from the lasers carrying the information between his brain and his computer to the neural receivers implanted just below his right ear to the computer itself—was tuned just right, Leif's entrance to veeyar made his head feel as if someone were trying to yank his brain right through the top of his skull.

Taking a deep breath, Leif opened his eyes to take in the computer reality he was visiting while his body rested back home in New York. He often thought that the monthly national get-togethers of the Net Force Explorers would be a lot more colorful if the members designed the meeting space. Certainly the local Net Force Explorers node was a sight to behold.

Instead, the national meetings usually took place in a government-issue veeyar built for practicality instead of flash. The walls kept expanding like the skin of a balloon, but they weren't being pushed outward by air molecules. The growing crowd of Net Force Explorers logging in kept the virtual room growing to hold them.

Leif always cut his schedule pretty fine when he arrived for meetings. Like all cybertravelers, theoretically he "moved" at the speed of light—or at least as close to it as the processing speed of the Net servers would let him. So it wasn't getting there that slowed him down. It was finding all the people he wanted to see and getting them together. He liked to show up on meeting night with just enough time to hook up with his friends before the business of the evening started.

This time around Matt Hunter was the first to spot Leif's thatch of red hair.

"So how are things in New York?" Matt asked, slipping his way through the crowd to stand at Leif's side. He hesitated for a moment. "Did Megan ever give you a copy of the captain's interview?"

"No, she did *not*," Leif said definitely. "I've gotten a couple of calls and a whole bunch of e-mail on the subject from nearly everybody I know. But when I asked Megan if I could see the actual show, you'd think I was asking for the filthiest of feelthy peectures."

Matt shrugged. "Well, the broadcast did get Megan— and a lot of other people, including Captain Winters— pretty upset."

"Upset doesn't quite cover it," Leif told him. "I finally decided to call the local HoloNews outlet. When I got hold of the switchboard and requested a copy, you'd have thought I'd initiated a level-three security breach."

That got a quick laugh from Matt. "A lot of the kids in this group have organized to express their . . . opinion— perhaps disapproval might be a better word—of the show."

He gave Leif a lopsided smile. "The station people have reason to act pretty defensive when it comes to callers about that show." Leif nodded.

"Particularly callers who sound on the young side."

Leif gave Matt a long look. "Normally, I'd pester David for the real story on the interview. But when I tried calling him, he said he was too busy to talk. I'd bet he's pretty involved in that 'disapproval' thing. Can you take me through what went down?"

Matt retold the story of the interview quickly. "Up to the end, it was a typical puff piece. 'What a nice civic group you've got here, Captain Winters.' Then the interviewer went into attack mode."

Matt paused for a second. "The guy must have been annoyed at the way Winters was handling him, because he made some snide comment about the captain being too cool. Then he asked if Winters knew about Stefano 'Steve the Bull' Alcista being paroled that day."

Matt looked sick. "From there on, it's sort of engraved in my memory. The news-drone asked, 'Isn't he the organized-crime figure who was accused of conspiracy and murder in the car-bombing that killed your wife?' "

"Whoa!" Leif burst out.

Matt nodded. "Guy's lucky that looks can't kill. Otherwise he'd have wound up as a burnt patch on the carpet. Captain Winters looked downright scary. I've known the man for years and never seen *anything* like it." Matt's voice went lower. "It was worse than scary, Leif. Winters looked as if he was fighting for control of his expression, muscle by muscle. But his eyes . . ." He shook his head. "I would not want *anyone* that angry at me, much less someone who looked as dangerous as Captain Winters looked at that moment."

Leif silently shook his head. "So there *was* a Mrs. Winters? It seems almost impossible to believe."

"They say it's Marine *sergeants* who grow from spores," Matt tried to joke. "Not officers."

Leif didn't even comment on Matt's jibe. He stuck with the topic at hand. "I always thought of the captain as—I dunno—*The Captain,* a work of art carved and perfected. Talking about him with a wife—somehow it just feels wrong. It's like talking about *The Thinker* being married." He gestured helplessly. "Just like I always think of Captain Winters being at work. It's hard to picture him goofing off, much less sharing his life with someone."

"Maybe he became all business after he lost his wife," Matt suggested.

A thoughtful light appeared in Leif's eyes. "You might be right. And this Alcista guy was supposed to be involved in her death?"

Matt's expression began to look worried. "Leif—you're not thinking—?"

That's the unfortunate part of having a reputation for plots and tricks, Leif thought. *Everybody expects you to jump right in and start being clever.*

He was glad of Matt's interruption when the other members of their crew came swarming around—at least, at first.

"Here's the guy we need!" Maj Green called out in her usual blunt way. "Leif will come up with something to make that news guy wish he'd never been born."

"What a wonderful idea—two wrongs to make a right. It's even traditional." David Gray sounded exasperated, as if this particular argument had been going on for some time.

"You want to turn the other cheek, Gray?" Maj retorted. "You'll probably end up with somebody's boot on it."

Leif was wondering how to calm them both down when a new interruption distracted everybody.

One of the virtual walls in this corner of government cyberspace suddenly retreated to create a small stage. Captain James Winters stood surveying the crowd of Net Force Explorers. If Leif had thought David was exasperated, Winters looked like he had the market cornered on the feeling—locked and loaded, squared and cubed.

Thanks to one of the small miracles of veeyar, the captain's voice drowned out all the other conversations, almost as if he were speaking through a heavy-duty PA system.

"Before I start this meeting officially," Winters said, "I want to devote a few words to my recent holo appearance—

or rather the reaction to it. This stuff has gotten way out of hand."

A protesting rumble came from the young Net Force Explorers, but Winters talked right over it. "HoloNews has temporarily suspended Mr. McGuffin's e-mail after all the spam and flame that ended up there. And I myself have had to delete Mr. McGuffin's personal address several times from the Net Force Explorer Net—even in nodes for chapters outside of D.C."

"I have a direct order to impart here," he said, stabbing his finger in the air, a short, emphatic gesture. "I'll be as plain as possible. Stop trying to punish Jay-Jay McGuffin."

"He pulled a lousy trick!" an angry voice rose from the crowd.

"Maybe. But he was doing his job—badly, I might agree—still, I knew I might end up tripping over a land mine when I went in there. It comes with the territory when you deal with the media. They want ratings, which means their shows—even the puff-piece shows—have to be exciting."

Winters took a deep breath. "Anyway, I would take it as a personal favor if you all left Mr. McGuffin alone."

His voice grew grimmer. "As for Stefano Alcista, his files are still under judicial lock, and I expect you to respect that. It's against the law to tamper with those files, and I know you'll keep that in mind. I am also sure that none of you would be *stupid* enough to try tangling with a professional criminal and known Mob insider. You'd end up worrying about a lot worse things than my reaction to an overeager reporter."

Leif stared as Winters's face became all planes and angles, as if the flesh had drawn tight over the bones of his skull. Wherever Winters had gone in thought in that instant, it was a mental landscape Leif hoped he never discovered himself. "I'd rather not have another person on my conscience when it comes to Steve the Bull."

Winters shook his head a little as if he was trying to fling that thought away. His voice changed, too, as he said, "Now that we've dealt with that, welcome to the national meeting of the Net Force Explorers, October 7, 2025." That was the official opening of the meeting. From this point on, everything would be recorded. The captain was clearly determined to route a path back to normalcy both for himself and for the Net Force Explorers, as quickly as possible.

Leif glanced around. Everyone was quiet as the captain dealt with various matters. By all appearances this was a typical meeting—just business as usual. But as the guest speaker was introduced, Leif couldn't help noticing the tension that remained in the air. He was reminded of an old saying of his father's: "You could cut the atmosphere with a knife." Right now, given the stress in this room, a chisel or laser—one with a lot of firepower—would be a more appropriate tool. Despite the captain's pleas, it was clear that this wasn't over, not by a long shot. Leif could only hope that nothing terrible would happen before it was.

3

Several days later Leif sat beside his father in the Andersons' living room, watching the family's holo system. A recording of the now-infamous Winters interview played to its end.

"I can see why Captain Winters got so upset on-camera," Magnus Anderson said. "Given the program, and the purported purpose of the interview, that was a pretty low blow, even for a would-be newshound. The captain made a pretty good recover, except for that single, unguarded moment."

"I'm just glad I finally got a chance to see what all the fuss is about." Leif glanced at his father. "Thanks for busting it out of Fortress HoloNews. I hope it wasn't a problem."

Magnus Anderson shrugged. Leif thought his dad looked a little embarrassed, which was odd. His father usually wasn't shy about using his wealth or position to get something when he felt the results justified the means.

"It just took a little honcho-to-honcho communication, calling in a few favors," his dad said. "Deborah Rockwell runs the Washington operation." He hesitated. "She used to be an on-air reporter, and I knew her."

Leif raised his eyebrows at the tone in his father's voice. "*Knew* her?"

An uncomfortable pause ensued.

"It was back in the dawn of time, before I met your mother," Magnus Anderson finally said. "We dated for a while."

"It all comes clear." Leif laughed. "You bummed a copy off an old girlfriend."

"Which might teach you something," his still-embarrassed father replied. "When you break up with someone, try to do it so that you keep a friend instead of making an enemy."

Now it was Leif's turn to be embarrassed. Leif's last relationship had been fairly tumultuous, and the resulting break-up had been a messy one. The girl in question had been a pretty but spoiled debutante far too used to getting her own way and having exactly what she wanted. By the time Leif figured this out, it was too late for him to simply disappear from the picture. When he had finally tired of catering to her every outrageous whim and had tried to distance himself gracefully, the results had been—well, Leif had seen Fourth of July celebrations with less fireworks. Both the spoiled debutante and her parents were *still* after his scalp.

Thankfully, his father changed the subject. "How much 'fuss' has this thing generated?" he asked, gesturing toward the holo display, which now showed Jay-Jay McGuffin moving on to his next guest. The newsman still looked disappointed that his final question hadn't rattled Winters into saying something inflammatory.

Little had McGuffin realized at that point what he had stirred up with his sledgehammer-style interview tactics. If he'd had the slightest inkling then of the trouble he was in for, he'd have looked nervous instead of disappointed.

"Fuss?" Leif said. "Oh, about as much as if that genius had rammed his face into a hornets' nest. The kids who saw the interview were calling those who hadn't while the show was still on. By evening every chapter of the Net Force Explorers in the country had heard of McGuffin's dirty trick. A fair number of the kids decided to get back at him."

"And how exactly was he stung?" Magnus Anderson wanted to know.

"At last count, about forty-five hundred phony subscriptions to various publications were entered in his name. He—um—'enrolled' in a lot of different newsgroups and got on a lot of e-mail lists," Leif said. "All of a sudden, he started getting recipes for rhubarb pies, begging letters from every charity known to mankind, and information from the Flat Earth Society. Entomologists Online was keeping him up to date on the latest in insect research, complete with detailed scenarios on the private lives of fruit flies. My favorite touch was the guy who volunteered him to the Amalgamated Historical Simulation Organizations. They were pretty surprised at Jay-Jay's registration form. Not too many people sign up to get virtually massacred by the Mongol hordes every time they go online."

His father silently shook his head.

"Well, you've got to give the kid who came up with that one credit for originality," Leif said. "I guess McGuffin wasn't as smart as he thought he was. Not when he chose to very publicly offend a guy with a couple of thousand protohacker friends."

"Especially when said friends are mostly under the age of seventeen," Magnus Anderson said dryly. He looked for a long moment at his son. "And you didn't get involved at all?"

Leif could understand his father's skeptical tone. After all, it wasn't so long ago that he'd gotten into big trouble for hacking into the private files of the *Washington Post* to help a Net Force Explorer friend. That had not, technically, been illegal. Leif had gotten the codes to get in. But it had been way over the line as far as his parents were concerned. And Leif had paid for it, big-time.

"I didn't do a thing," Leif told his father, trying to look as virtuous as possible. "I've learned lately to look before I leap."

Leif didn't mention that he'd been out the night that the

"Get McGuffin!" campaign had started. Or that, when he'd finally checked his e-mail messages, all the best cybervengeance schemes had been used already.

"How about this other character?" Magnus Anderson asked. "The gangster—Alcista?"

"Net Force Explorers are not stupid. Even we know he's out of our league. Besides, Winters personally asked us to butt out. No more ragging on McGuffin, and absolutely no fooling around with Alcista."

Leif's father nodded. "What's the old quote? 'Leave him to heaven.' "

"Shakespeare," Leif said. "And it's 'Leave *her* to heaven.' The ghost says it in Act One of *Hamlet.*"

Magnus Anderson gave his son one of those looks. "Well, at least you're learning *something* while you're giving your mother and me gray hair."

Leif had nothing to say to that. Luckily, he also had a distraction. "My wallet-phone just went off," he said, reaching into his back pocket.

It only took a moment to convert the wallet's circuitry. Leif held the foilpack phone up to his ear. "Hello? Matt! What are you—?"

That was as far as he got. Leif sat for a long moment, listening, his face going grimmer with every word he heard.

"Yeah. I don't think it would have made the New York news, either. Thanks for letting me know." He sighed. "Maybe this will mean the end of all this nonsense. We can only hope so, at any rate."

Leif said goodbye to Matt Hunter, then cut the connection.

Magnus Anderson looked carefully at his son. "A problem?" he asked.

"Looks as if someone decided to ignore both Shakespeare *and* Captain Winters," Leif said. "According to Washington HoloNews, Steve the Bull Alcista got into his car earlier this evening, and it blew up with him inside it. He's history."

•   •   •

Guess you can't be lucky all the time, Matt Hunter thought a couple of days later as he sat in front of his family's holo system. Steve the Bull's release from prison had been lost among a flurry of hot news items. But the Alcista murder happened on a slow news day. Leif had called him to report that Alcista's death had indeed made the New York newscasts, even led off a couple of the shows. The story was national.

Even now, two days later, interest was still high. The top HoloNews magazine show, *Once Around the Clock,* had done a special report on the New Mafia. Several reporters hosted segments on the computer-literate leaders who had arisen from old-style crime families to take advantage of the criminal aspects of the Net. In these segments Steve the Bull was depicted as a throwback to the pre-Net days, too quick with his trigger finger to succeed in the new criminal empire.

Then Tori Rush came on. She was the latest addition to the staff of the newsmagazine, with only a couple of years on the air under her belt. Blond and petite, she looked like America's kid sister—America's *sexy* kid sister.

But she certainly wasn't very cute and cuddly right now. Her story was an exposé on the bombing of Alcista's car. And she was questioning the current police theory that Alcista's murder was an organized-crime hit. Tori had done her homework—she'd gone all the way back to the case that had put the crime boss in jail this time: the computer-driven looting of a legitimate corporation.

In addition to background information on the case itself, she had a lot of footage about how Alcista had allegedly tried to kill the pair of Net Force agents investigating that case. Alcista or one of his minions had supposedly rigged the Net Force agents' vehicles with car bombs.

Tori Rush's slightly pouty lips formed a hard, thin line as she went into crusading-reporter mode. "The charges that Alcista planted the devices were, in the end, never successfully proved in a court of law, but the bombs were a definite fact. One Net Force agent lost his wife as a result of them." The hologram image filled with a photo—a younger James Winters with a pretty dark-haired woman holding on to his arm.

"Cynthia Winters drove her husband's car on the morning of Monday, April 19, 2021. The bomb wired to the ignition killed her instantly. It has been more than four years since that terrible incident. But it's safe to say that Net Force Captain James Winters hasn't forgotten, as this recent interview shows."

Matt's skin crawled as a familiar scene appeared on the display. Jay-Jay McGuffin asked Captain Winters how he felt about Steve the Bull Alcista getting out of prison.

The image zoomed in and froze on the raw rage engraved on the captain's face.

Then the terrifying close-up of James Winters was replaced by the image of Tori Rush, looking very serious.

"New Mafia or not," she said, "it might be wise to remember that Stefano Alcista's enemies are not all criminals."

Tori's segment ended, and an ad came on. But Matt Hunter still faced the holo set, feeling slightly numb.

I always thought Tori Rush was kind of hot, he thought. *Not anymore. If she could do that to the captain, she's cold.* He shuddered. *Cold as ice.*

Megan O'Malley blinked through her connection to the Net—and opened her eyes to the virtual meeting hall of the Net Force Explorers. The crowd was bigger than usual, so she had a bit of a job finding her friends. And when she did, none of them—not even Mark Gridley—could explain why a special national meeting had been called.

At eight o'clock on the dot one of the walls receded to create a small stage where James Winters stood. But he wasn't alone.

"Dad!" Mark Gridley blurted out. Jay Gridley, the head of Net Force, stood beside him. Behind them were two more men—strangers.

"Welcome to this special meeting of the Net Force Explorers." Captain Winters followed his usual ritual for officially starting a meeting, then hesitated. "I think I'll let the boss take over from here," he said.

Jay Gridley stepped forward. "Captain Winters suggested this meeting, and asked that I be here so that you'd be the first to hear about this situation—and you'd get the story straight from the source, without any exaggerations or distortions."

"What situation?" Megan hissed at Mark Gridley. "What story?"

All she got was a baffled shrug in reply.

"Last night a national newsmagazine broadcast raised certain questions about one of our agents," Gridley went on. "I don't think those questions are valid, but for the good of the agency I do think they should be answered fully. So I've asked Hank Steadman, the head of our Internal Affairs division, to conduct an investigation of that agent."

"Hangman Hank, that's what I've heard the regular agents call him," Megan heard somebody mutter in the crowd. "He's head of the rat squad."

The older of the two other men on the virtual stage stepped forward. "My people will try to do their jobs as quickly and unobtrusively as possible," Steadman said. "But it's official Net Force policy that while the investigation goes on, the agent under investigation, Captain James Winters, will remain off duty."

A storm of murmured protest broke out among the Net Force Explorers at this announcement. Captain Winters took the podium and raised his voice. "I realize this is going to be tough on you, just as it's tough on me. And I'm touched by your loyalty. But rules are rules, and I can hardly ask you to remember that axiom if I don't follow it myself. This is the way things have to be," he said, "while Captain Steadman makes his necessary, routine . . . and hopefully brief . . . investigation."

Jay Gridley gave a quick, emphatic nod.

Megan noticed, however, that "Hangman Hank" Steadman's nod wasn't as positive.

Jay Gridley took over the meeting again. "Think of it as Captain Winters finally being able to take some vacation time. We all know how hard the man works. A little peace will do him good," he said. "While Captain Winters is away, your Net Force Explorers liaison will be Agent Len Dorpff."

Megan finally turned her attention to the fourth man on the stage. Compared to the rest of the men, Agent Len Dorpff looked like a kid. In fact, several of the kids in the crowd facing the podium looked older than he did. Dorpff had an eager, awkward kind of face. With freckles. Worst of all, at least from Megan's point of view, his ears stuck out.

"Agent?" David Gray muttered in scorn as he looked at the man. "He doesn't look old enough to have finished college, much less the FBI Academy. Looks to me like Net Force scraped the bottom of the barrel to come up with him."

"Looks like it," Leif Anderson agreed. "In Gridley's defense, it *was* short notice, and a temporary assignment at that. He probably didn't want to put someone too valuable into the position."

Dorpff stepped out front and center, like a cadet about to speak to his class.

"Men," he began. Then he broke off, his face going a dull red as he scanned his audience. Roughly half the kids there—maybe more—were girls. Megan wasn't the only girl who bristled at the agent's unthinking comment.

"People," Dorpff hastily changed his opening. "Young . . . people."

He's babbling, Megan thought.

The young agent finally got back to his prepared speech, seemingly grabbing at his cue cards like a drowning man at a lifeline. "I'll be stepping into some pretty big shoes for this assignment, but Captain Winters has been kind enough to brief me—"

"Clearly not enough," a female voice said with enough volume to make Dorpff blush again.

"I hope we'll be able to work together to keep things running during the captain's absence." Dorpff's words came out in a desperate rush.

Megan glanced around at her friends, who looked about

as stunned and unhappy as she did. She didn't care how old Dorpff was or what he looked like as long as he was up to the job. But Megan wasn't sensing a confortable level of competence about this man. He was in over his head and going down three times—almost before he even started.

We've got to do something, she thought. *With this clown running things, the Explorers won't last a week!*

4

The crew that Megan liked to think of as the "D.C. Nine" got together after the surprise Net Force Explorers meeting to talk. Matt Hunter's virtual workspace was as crowded as the O'Malley living room had been during the broadcast of Winters's interview—although, thanks to the miracle of Net technology, the visitors didn't have to worry about having enough chairs to sit on or space to park them in. Megan, Andy Moore, Maj Green, David Gray, Catie Murray, Daniel Sanchez, and Mark Gridley floated among clouds and stars around the unsupported marble platform Matt was using as a desk these days.

The non-Washington members of the group were a bit later linking in. Leif was in New York City, but he appeared virtually in Matt's space soon enough, rubbing the sides of his head as he took his place in the crowd. P. J. Farris was in Texas with his father. He was the last to "arrive," dressed in the boots, brush-popper shirt, and blue jeans he often wore when he was on his family's ranch.

Even though Matt was the one who had invited everyone in, Megan started the ball rolling. "I can't believe anybody here is happy with the dimwit they brought in to replace the captain," she said.

"Tell us about it," Maj grumbled. "Why would they bring in somebody so wet behind his ears? From the way he shot himself in the foot just by opening his mouth today, you have to wonder what he was like on the firing range."

Megan was in no mood for joking. She came right out with what was on her mind. "We've got to do something to get Captain Winters out of trouble and send Agent *Dork* back wherever he came from."

"It's just for a little while," Matt pointed out.

"Yeah?" Megan shot back. "Then how come nobody mentioned exactly how long that 'little while' would be? If this was going to be an open-and-shut sort of investigation, wouldn't somebody have given us an estimated time of completion? And even though Winters tried to pass it off as a pain-in-the-butt standard annoyance, I noticed that 'Hangman Hank' Steadman didn't lighten up. He looked about as serious as a hearse throughout the whole thing."

"Megan, you're making it sound like Winters is going to be fired," Mark Gridley protested. "My dad would never—"

Megan cut him off. "A week ago, you'd have told me your dad would never have suspended the captain."

Mark opened his mouth, then shut it.

"So what are you suggesting, Megan?" Andy wanted to know. "You thinking of sending nasty e-mail to Jay Gridley? That would be kind of cool—trying to flame the head of Net Force—"

"For however long you got away with it," David, the usual voice of reason, cut in. "I figure the FBI would be knocking on your door in about fifteen minutes."

"I don't think that's the way—" Matt began.

"So we're just supposed to sit like statues while Captain Winters gets crucified?" Megan demanded. She rounded on Mark before he could even speak. "And don't try telling me about how he'll be protected. The minute Tori Rush put the story on *Once Around the Clock*, it became political. And everybody knows how politics runs in this city."

"Okay, then. What can we do?" Leif Anderson asked sarcastically. "Are we supposed to turn the reign of terror from whatsisname—that McGuffin guy—to this news-babe instead?"

Megan didn't have an answer, and Matt jumped in. "Now, wait a *minute!*" he said. "The captain asked us specifically to leave McGuffin alone. If we do anything to a network newsperson, it will just make matters worse for Captain Winters."

"But we've got to do *something*," Daniel Sanchez said. "Maybe you guys can afford to blow off an adult who believes in us—who listens and tries to help out. *I* can't."

Megan glanced at this unexpected ally. She knew that Daniel had a tough family situation—a lot rougher than anyone else in this group. But he had a point. Most of the kids in this room were able to depend on their parents and some of their teachers in a pinch. But none of the kids had enough adults they could count on to back them in a tough spot that they could afford to lose one.

Even Matt was silenced by Daniel's words. He thought for a second, and a glimmer of an idea began to form. "Maybe we can do something to show that we back Captain Winters one hundred percent," he said. "Even the captain couldn't complain about us showing our opinion of him—as long as we don't go after someone else."

"That sounds good, but I don't think it goes far enough. The HoloNews network headquarters is up in New York," Leif said. "Maybe I can poke around up there and see what's going on."

"I want to help, too," Mark Gridley unexpectedly spoke up. "I could try to get into Dad's files and find out how the investigation is going."

"You sure you want to do that?" David Gray's expression was serious as he looked down at the Squirt.

The younger boy merely nodded. "Yeah, I know. Spying on the head of Net Force. It's probably fairly high on the 'not a bright idea' list." Mark's round, tanned face suddenly tightened. "But even if I get caught, what's Dad going to do to me? Especially when I tell him why I did it. I'm pretty sure it'll be all right, as long as we don't try anything nasty."

Megan looked around at the others, strong emotion momentarily robbing her of her voice. She cleared her throat. "That's not going to be enough," she finally said. "None of it is. I've been doing some research on Hangman Hank. He used to be with the FBI until he was brought into Net Force a year ago. Apparently, one of the higher-ups in the FBI thought at the time that Net Force's internal affairs needed tightening up. You know how it is. Computer types never look buttoned down enough to government bigwigs. Or, more likely, maybe the FBI just wanted to get rid of the guy. Jay Gridley's tried to get him moved somewhere else, but the man's got good connections. He's a political appointee, the kind that's tough to get shed of. Anyway, this guy's never been a field agent, even in the FBI. He's always specialized in internal security and investigations. And he always gets *something* on the people he investigates. It's his theory that nobody has clean hands. And maybe he's right. You can't be out on the streets as a field agent and run things one hundred percent by the book all the time."

The others didn't say anything. But she could see from their faces that this was something they'd already heard or at least suspected. After all, how many times had they jumped into action because the hands of Net Force were officially tied? Even though they knew he was innocent, Captain Winters could be in serious trouble if the Internal Affairs department decided to go on a witch hunt.

"With Steadman on your case, if you're lucky, you either wind up humiliated or with a wrecked career. If you aren't lucky, you end up behind bars. And he's going to go all-out on a high-profile case like this one."

"We're with you," Leif said. "What can we do to help?"

She blinked, hoping to hide the tears that suddenly sprang to her eyes. "Do you think the piddling stuff we're offering to do will really help?"

Megan didn't allow herself to wait for an answer. Choking back her frustration and fear, she cut the connection and vanished from Matt's space.

Seconds later Matt floated open-mouthed in his virtual workspace, staring at the spot where Megan had stood.

"Well," Leif said, "that was a bit more exciting than most of our after-meeting get-togethers."

"Even more exciting than most meetings I've been to," Mark agreed. He made a production of looking at the virtual watch on his wrist. "Maybe I should be heading out, too."

"You really going to do what you said you would?" Andy Moore asked.

Offended, Mark gave him a quick look. "I *said* I would." Then he vanished, too.

Mark's exit seemed to open the door for everybody else. A couple of people, David Gray among them, apologized as they left. Matt didn't say much to them as they vanished, one after another. After Megan's outburst, what more was there left to say?

Soon Matt's virtual sanctum was empty except for himself and Leif Anderson.

"I thought you'd be in a hurry to pull out and begin your investigation of Tori Rush." Matt couldn't keep the bitterness out of his voice. "Maybe you'll discover she was a centerfold model before she went into news. That way we'll have some interesting pictures to look at—even if Captain Winters gets shafted."

"I don't think Tori Rush will be that easy a nut to crack," Leif said. "At best, I'm hoping all her innuendos will turn out to be nothing."

"But that didn't stop you from stepping in and giving Megan a little backup there."

Leif just raised his eyebrows. "Yeah. And you saw how much she thanked me for it." He sighed. "No matter what we do, I know Megan's going to be stirring things up, pushing the envelope to help the captain. As long as she thinks some of us might help her, at least she'll stay in touch. And that's a good thing. We don't need her out there as a loose cannon."

Matt shuddered. "Okay. You've got a point there." He turned troubled eyes toward Leif. "But you were at the last meeting—the last *regular* meeting—where Captain Winters asked us to lay off."

"He asked us to lay off McGuffin, and not to mess around with Steve the Bull Alcista." Leif spread his hands, the picture of innocence. "And I *will* observe those requests. I'm not going near either of them. Neither are you."

Matt had to laugh. "When the time comes for you to decide what you're going to be when you grow up, you should consider being a lawyer." He shook his head. "Or, as my Irish grandmother pronounces it, a *liar.*"

Leif gave him a thin-lipped smile. "It's a possibility," he said. "Do you have any ideas on what we as a group can do to tell Winters we all still love him?"

"Nothing very definite—or very helpful," Matt admitted. "A picket line with a couple of cardboard signs would look more pathetic than supportive. And where would we go? The HoloNews office here in D.C.? Their headquarters in your town?" He managed a sour smile. "Or maybe Jay Gridley's office?"

"Hangman Hank Steadman's office." Leif's grin was wicked. "He'd love the media coverage." Then he got more serious. "I'll bet it's not just the kids here who'd want to help. We'll want to do something national—something on the Net."

"You think I can get David to hack in and stick a message of support on all of America's phone bills?" Matt suggested.

Leif laughed. "A little extreme, maybe, but I think you're heading in the right direction."

The humorous glint in Matt's eyes faded. "Watching that meeting last night—it was like being told that Captain Winters had contracted some terrible disease. I just want to send him a giant get-well card."

"Why don't you?" Leif said. "Draft up a petition, something like that, and send it out to all the chapters. See if you can get every member to sign on." He shrugged. "It shouldn't be too hard. Look how quickly you guys got things rolling when you began banging the drums to roast Jay-Jay McGuffin's tail."

Matt slowly nodded. "You may have something there. Not exactly a petition, but a statement of support from all the Net Force Explorers, individually and together."

Leif shrugged. "I'd sign it."

Matt looked at him. "And to tell the truth, that sort of surprises me. The captain has roasted *your* tail from time to time over some of the stuff you've pulled. He trusts you only about as far as he can throw you."

Leif wasn't smiling at all as he leaned forward. "Look, I really like Captain Winters. Maybe it's because of that suspicion, that continuous back and forth when we talk. I respect him for it. He's usually right, too. I almost always *am* up to something when he thinks I am. Or maybe it's something more than that. Remember what Daniel said? How he likes Captain Winters because the captain believes in him? Well, you've got to believe in something in this life. Me, I believe in James Winters."

Leif looked a little embarrassed, as if he'd said something he shouldn't. "Do me a favor and don't spread that around, okay? It would ruin my rep as a cool, cynical playboy-in-training."

"Yeah, right," Matt muttered as his friend finally blinked out of his space. "That rep fits you to a T."

Matt's "giant get-well card" project succeeded far beyond anything he'd expected. All the local chapters enthusiastically jumped on board when he contacted them. Signatures began pouring in for his statement of support. Even kids who hadn't been reporting in for meetings lately—including a few kids who'd been in the hospital—signed on to help Captain Winters. In days Matt had the signatures of every recorded Net Force Explorer.

That was the good part. Then he realized he had to get these signatures organized somehow and get them to Net Force and James Winters. Sorting the names against membership data, he got the signatures organized into local groups. Once he had the presentation problem licked, then there was the problem of delivery.

Jay Gridley's office was easy. All it took was a phone call to Mark to get that Net address. But Captain Winters was a tougher nut to crack. With the captain suspended, it didn't seem very likely he'd be checking his office e-mail. And when Matt tracked down a personal Net address for a J. Winters that looked promising, he got no response. The captain didn't answer his home phone, either.

Matt couldn't say he was exactly surprised. Since Tori Rush's piece on *Once Around the Clock,* there had been a steadily growing media circus focused on the car bombings, both the recent one and the older ones. And the center ring of that circus was the alleged Alcista-Winters murder case. With reporters asking him repeatedly for comments and answers to questions, the captain probably had good reasons not to pick up when his phone bleated.

But it also meant that Matt couldn't warn Winters that a special message was on the way from the Explorers. And that meant he couldn't depend on sending off the petition electronically.

No, he would have to resort to a hard copy or a datascrip, delivered by hand. Matt spent a day reworking his document, decided how he wanted the final document to look, then tracked down a service bureau to print it out. The message was too massive to manage on his home system. He wanted the statement and signatures to appear in full color all on one piece of paper, and that meant finding a company that still used printers with paper rolls.

David Gray helped in the search, and Matt finally found a place that could handle the job. A few hours later he headed off with the result of his efforts—a very bulky roll of paper—under his arm. As he came out of a suburban Metro station, Matt hailed a cab in the parking lot and gave the driver James Winters's home address. He winced when he heard the fare. This hand-delivery stuff didn't just take time out of his day. It meant shelling out some serious money, too. But Captain Winters was worth it. Besides, if costs got out of hand, Matt knew he could get Leif to foot some of the bill.

He looked out the window as he rolled along en route to the captain's house. It was a pleasant neighborhood, with good-sized houses spaced well apart. There was lots of room for front and back yards. Young kids were playing in several of those yards. Matt passed a little girl riding on a bicycle, and some guys shooting hoops on a backboard attached over a garage.

Matt blinked. He hadn't really given much thought to how the captain lived outside of work. Maybe it was Winters's military facade. But Matt somehow thought of his mentor in relation to offices or barracks, not as a suburb-dweller.

When he pulled up at the appropriate address, Matt didn't expect to see the paneled Colonial-style house overlooking a good stretch of woods. But there was no mistaking the place. This was Captain Winters's home, all right. The media vans parked across the street were a dead giveaway. Several vaguely official-looking vans were parked in the driveway. And James Winters stood in the driveway with Captain Hank Steadman of Net Force Internal Affairs.

They both turned suspicious eyes on the cab as it pulled up to the place.

They're probably expecting some idiot reporter to pop out, Matt thought. He wished again he'd been able to call ahead. No way did he want to intrude on the investigation.

But Captain Winters smiled in welcome when Matt emerged from his cab.

"Matt!" he said in surprise. Then he turned to Steadman. "This is one of my Net Force Explorers, Matt Hunter. What brings you out here, Matt?"

Steadman excused himself and headed for the garage as Matt presented his printout. Winters read the statement of support with his usual quiet, serious expression. But Matt thought there was a hint of mist in the captain's eyes as he partially unrolled the paper to see the beginning of the list of signatures in three neat rows, then hefted the weight of the scroll in his hand to get some idea of how very long the list was.

"Every current Net Force Explorer signed," Matt said with pride, "as well as some kids who aren't with the group anymore, either because they graduated from the program or went on to pursue other interests."

"Matt—" Winters had to clear his throat before he went on. "Thank you. This couldn't have come at a better time. It's not a pleasant experience to have your colleagues execute a search warrant on your house."

"It's a nice-looking place," Matt said.

Winters glanced at him, a hint of a smile quirking his lips. "What? You were expecting a cave? Or maybe a bunker? What a disappointment! The captain lives in a house!" Winters shrugged. "I try to keep it neat. And I *know* it's clean."

Matt sensed immediately that Winters wasn't referring to his housekeeping skills.

Hangman Hank Steadman came back out of the garage, his eyes hooded. "Captain," he said formally, "you told us you hadn't used the workshop back there for quite some time."

"It's been months," Winters replied. "I was cutting some wood during the summer to make repairs on the deck out back."

Steadman gave him a brief, almost ironic, nod. "In that case, can you explain why there's no dust on any of the tools in there?" The IA man pressed on. "And why we found traces of plastic explosive on your workbench?"

5

Matt stepped into Captain Winters's office—he still couldn't think of it in any other way—and shook hands with Agent Dorpff.

"Matt Hunter?" The youthful-looking agent smiled. "Good to start meeting some of the guys—and girls—in the organization," he quickly added, obviously remembering his disastrous introduction to the Net Force Explorers. "Captain Winters specifically mentioned you as part of what he called 'the local organizational cadre,'" Dorpff went on.

"Really?" Matt said, a little flattered.

Agent Dorpff nodded. "Looks like the captain was right," he said. "Considering the job you did on that petition. A nationwide response in less than a week!"

He gave an embarrassed shrug at Matt's look of surprise. "Hey, it's part of my job, checking out what's happening on the Net Force Explorer Net."

Dorpff looked concerned. "I hope you weren't too upset by what happened when you went to deliver the printout."

Matt couldn't help himself. "How did you—"

His answer was another shrug. "I may be the guy on the

bottom of the organizational totem pole, but even I hear things," Dorpff said.

"And is this part of the job, too?" Matt asked. "Consoling the upset teenagers?"

"It's probably in the job description somewhere," Dorpff said. "But even though I'm just starting out, I'm not stupid enough to think that you'll forget Captain Winters." He hesitated for a second. "I do want you to know that I'll be there . . . if you need me."

"In case I've scarred my poor psyche?" Matt said. "Hey, all I did was see a bunch of lab nerds running around in the captain's garage."

"So you actually got to see the workshop?" Dorpff said.

"From the garage door," Matt said. "It looked clean."

"Clean as a whistle, from what I heard." The young agent frowned. "I always wondered, why would anyone consider a whistle particularly clean? It would be full of spit and germs—"

Matt didn't let him change the subject. "Maybe Winters has the world's most fanatical cleaning lady."

"A suspicious mind would think in terms of an attempt to destroy evidence," Dorpff replied. "Even so, those lab nerds found indications of Semtec, a fine, old-fashioned plastic explosive still used in some military munitions. And from the trace chemicals they put in the stuff—taggants, they're called—it was linked to a batch of the stuff involved in one of the captain's old cases." Dorpff shrugged. "You hear about people taking their work home, but even so—"

"Very funny," Matt said.

"Here's something not so funny," the young agent went on. "The same chemical tracers were found in the bomb that blew up Stefano Alcista."

Matt stared as if Dorpff had just punched him in the gut.

"The captain said he hadn't been in the workshop in months," Matt said. "And knowing how busy the job keeps him, I have no problem believing that's true. There've been times when kids have called this office late, or even on the weekend, and found him in—"

"But, oddly, he wasn't in the office most of the afternoon before the Alcista bombing," Dorpff interrupted almost gently. "He claimed he'd gotten a call to meet an informant who never showed. But there's no record of such a call. Captain Winters left at two P.M. and didn't get back until four forty-five. Less than an hour later Steve the Bull decides to go for a car ride, and . . . boom!"

"It's not *that* much time," Matt argued desperately. "In some companies that would be considered a long lunch hour."

Dorpff nodded. "And street informants have a pretty elastic sense of time—when they even bother to show. But there was no phone call on record here, either to the captain's desk or to his foilpack."

The agent looked at Matt for a long moment. "Do you know about the MOM theory of crime?"

"Um—what?" Matt said, expecting some bizarre psychological mumbo-jumbo about mother fixations. Frankly, he had a harder time imagining Winters with a mother than he did thinking of the captain as being married. The captain was so emotionally mature it was hard to think of him as a drooling toddler.

"It's an old acronym for the main elements in investigating a crime," Dorpff explained. "Motive, Opportunity, and Means. M-O-M. Put your feelings for Captain Winters aside for a moment and consider how the elements line up in this case."

He ticked off one finger. "Motive—that's pretty obvious. Alcista is believed to be behind the death of Captain Winters's wife. And half the world has seen that news segment, showing the look on Winters's face when he heard about Alcista getting out. I think we can take motive for granted."

Matt gave a stiff-necked nod.

Dorpff held up a second finger. "Opportunity. Winters disappears from his office for several hours the day Alcista dies. The captain doesn't have a satisfactory reason why he was missing. And the part of the story we *can* check out— the phone call from the informant—doesn't check out."

"I bet a lot of people were out of the office," Matt said.

"And the call could have come in on a line other than the direct one to Winters's desk and been forwarded. That happens all the time. Are they checking on that?"

"Yes, but there's no denying the captain had the opportunity to commit the crime. That's where MOM comes in," Dorpff pointed out. "We're interested right now only in the people who have a motive for hurting Alcista."

He hesitated, then put up a third finger. "Finally—means. Steve the Bull was nailed by a Semtec bomb. Traces of the same batch of Semtec turn up in Captain Winters's home workshop."

The young agent hesitated again. "I probably shouldn't tell you this, but it will undoubtedly leak out soon enough. Internal Affairs ran a Net search of suspicious occurrences near the captain's home. They found a police report in the next township. Somebody had complained about an explosion in a patch of woods two days before Alcista went to meet his maker. When Steadman's techs checked the site, they found a crater—and the remains of a Semtec bomb. Sort of a trial run, you might say. Working out the bugs. And the bomb had definite problems. There were large fragments that hadn't been vaporized. The lab boys think they can get fingerprints—"

Dorpff broke off, giving Matt a look of what could only be interpreted as pity. "I know you admire Captain Winters, Matt. You and the other Net Force Explorers have shown a hundred-percent loyalty to the man. You're all outraged that this should be happening to your friend and mentor."

The agent's face looked even younger as he leaned across Captain Winters's desk, his expression pained and earnest. "I didn't know the man—we only had a brief meeting while he brought me up to speed on the Net Force Explorers. But I could see he thought the world of you kids."

Dorpff took a deep breath, then let it out as a sigh. "There's a definite case against Captain Winters. Maybe it would be best for both sides if you at least considered the possibility that he might be guilty of the things he's being accused of."

• • •

"Can you believe it?" Matt stormed. His figure went in and out of Leif Anderson's sight as Matt strode back and forth in front of his holo pickup. "That jug-eared idiot was trying to break it to me gently that Captain Winters was guilty! Based on a case that's completely—completely—" He broke off, searching for a word.

"Circumstantial?" Leif suggested.

" 'Lame' is closer to an honest description," Matt replied in exasperation. "I mean, the captain is supposed to be a top Net Force agent, right? He was apparently a legendary field man—one of the best. But he seems to have packed his brains in deep storage while he was planning this crime he's accused of."

"You'd think the captain would know about this Motive, Opportunity, and Means stuff," Leif agreed. "Dorpff isn't bright enough to invent it on his own, so they must teach it at the Academy."

"So, knowing how Net Force will investigate, of course the first thing the captain would do is build a bomb in his garage, where traces are sure to be found," Matt said angrily. "And then he'd test it the next town over, because of course he'd forget about any Net searches for suspicious connections. Finally he'd openly leave the office to attach the new, improved bomb to Alcista's car—and not bother to give himself a respectable alibi."

"When you put it that way, it does sound pretty ridiculous," Leif said. "But remember the look on the captain's face. Could *you* be that angry and think clearly?"

"I think any Net Force agent could. I certainly think the captain could. At the very least, he'd have to realize his appearance on that show painted a big 'Motive' sign on his forehead."

"So your theory boils down to this. If Winters killed this guy, he'd have done a smarter job of it," Leif finally said.

"Exactly," Matt replied. When he realized what he'd said, he began rubbing his forehead. "But if I have to start convincing you . . ."

"No, I see your point," Leif interrupted. "And I agree with it."

"You're about the only one." Matt didn't meet his friend's eyes. "I couldn't convince Agent Dork. And I got bad news from the Squirt. Mark says it feels as if someone died over at his house. His parents are both awfully upset, and they won't talk about Captain Winters's situation with him."

Leif nodded. "I'm sure Jay Gridley is getting enough of those sorts of discussions on the job," he said. "Winters has always seemed to me to be very well-liked by his fellow agents. I have noticed lately that Gridley's statements to the press have become progressively more careful."

"More cagey, you mean," Matt spat the words. "Megan really called it this time. She said that as soon as the captain's picture got spread all over the news, the case would become political. It must be getting really bad if Jay Gridley is picking his words."

He was silent for a moment, then looked at Leif. "Looks as if this will take a lot more than statements of support. Winters is in big trouble."

"Now I get it," Leif said. "Things are getting out of hand, so you call in your pal the scamologist to see if he can't come up with something—what? Clever? Devious? Certainly something that Captain Winters would never approve of—if he heard about it."

"Leif, we've got to do something," Matt said in a small voice. "This whole trail of evidence . . . I'm convinced someone is trying to frame the captain."

"You may be right. I'll see what I can do," Leif replied gruffly. "Call you soon."

The holographic link broke, and Leif sent a twisted grin in the direction of the pickup. He didn't want to tell Matt, in case things didn't work out.

But he already had something in the works.

The smoky room vibrated in time to the bass beat of the band's pounding rock rhythm.

Leif took a deep breath—and coughed. The place was

called Club Retro, and it was one of the hottest spots in New York City right now. He wasn't sure why. Virtual reality had created a world where, just by plumping down on a computer-link couch, you could become anybody and go anywhere. So, of course, everybody who was anybody was going to this dingy basement in real life. It was cool. It was different.

Actually, in Leif's opinion, it was hot and kind of choking. The pile-driver thump of the bass hit Leif like a physical attack. *Could this stuff knock my implant circuitry loose from my skull?* he thought.

Spotlights located on the ceilings flashed on and off, and some sort of lasers flickered over the crowd. It looked just like a holo of an old 1990s club. Of course, that was what Club Retro was built to look like. The unpredictable lighting flashed down on a swirling crowd of dancers, turning their flesh a sort of icy blue.

It wasn't going to be easy to find the person he was looking for here.

But Leif was lucky. He found Alexis de Courcy at the foot of the improbable silver staircase that led to the dance floor. Alexis was Leif's height. But he had a couple of years on Leif, not to mention dark, carefully styled hair and deeply tanned, perfect features. Alexis often talked about the great days of "Eurotrash" and "the Jet Set" and he always wore the most extreme fashions, drove the hottest cars . . . and pursued the wildest adventures. When he saw Leif, Alexis took a sip from a glass that seemed to be smoking, and grinned.

"Mon ami," the French boy began, "you owe me for this one."

"As long as my father doesn't cut the credit cards," Leif replied, "you've got it."

"You'll pay in more ways than that," Alexis said. "I found a perfect connection for you. But she's—what's the old phrase? Ah, yes. 'High maintenance.' "

"As long as she's an intern at HoloNews," Leif said.

"Oh, the young woman is all that and more," Alexis said. "You're in for an interesting time."

"You didn't lay it on too thick?" Leif asked, suddenly nervous as he followed Alexis through the club.

"Actually, I told a surprising amount of the truth," Alexis replied. "Your father is rich, and he is Swedish. Just a few small details are off. She thinks you're Swedish, too, in the big city for a hot time. She thinks your name is Leif Magnuson—I thought that was rather clever. More or less true, as well. And, of course, she thinks you're somewhat older than you actually are. The young lady wouldn't be caught dead with 'some high-school guy.' "

The flat accent Alexis adopted made Leif suspect his friend was actually mimicking tonight's target.

Alexis nodded. "There she is."

The girl was short and curvy, dressed in the present fashion uniform for the trendy young woman; something called the preppy bad-girl look. A low cut, oversized sweater nearly hid the tiny pleated skirt she wore. The girl's wild mane of red curls grew even wilder as she whipped her head around as she danced.

When the music stopped, Alexis beckoned her over. "Bodie, this is the friend I was talking about. Leif Magnuson, Bodie Fuhrman."

Leif took her very warm hand. "A pleasure," he said, putting on his European manners and a slight Swedish accent. "Did I hear correctly? Bodie?"

"Short for Boadicea, the ancient queen who almost threw the Romans out of Britain." Bodie Fuhrman had obviously made this explanation many times before. "Mom decided to name all her daughters after great women in history. On the luck scale, I sort of fall between my big sister Nefertiti and the kid of my family, Marie Curie Fuhrman."

"Charming," Leif assured her.

"Yeah, Bodie the Body, that's me." The girl wiggled in time to the next tune. The implication was clear. She wasn't exactly the shyest of young women.

"I am afraid my family is much more conservative," Leif said. "I have been allowed to take a year away from the university to travel and learn about my father's business."

"Wish I could do that," Bodie said. "I'm busting my buns

at Columbia and holding down an internship at HoloNews."

"It sounds like interesting work." Leif wasn't sure whether he should press for more details or spend a little more time charming the girl.

"That's what I thought when I started out," Bodie shrugged. "But for all its sources, HoloNews apparently hasn't heard the news about the slaves being freed. And I work for the worst slave driver of them all, the news goddess—Tori Rush."

6

Leif danced with Bodie Fuhrman, enjoying her moves. She was an energetic, almost reckless dancer, a young woman who moved the way *she* wanted to move. Several times Leif found himself having to duck if he wanted to avoid a flailing arm or a bumping hip.

By the time the music ended, Bodie had a faint sheen on her face and a twinkle in her emerald-green eyes. " 'Wild and crazy,' that's what everybody says about me." She giggled.

"It just gives me something to keep up with," Leif replied with a smile.

After a couple more wild dances, Bodie decided she needed a drink. Leif bought a simple soda. Bodie asked for one of those foaming, smoking concoctions that Alexis had been drinking.

Time to make my move, Leif thought. "So you work for the famous Tori Rush," he said.

"I don't know how famous she is in Sweden," Bodie said, breathing out a puff of smoke. "But she's a pretty big cheese over here. Just ask her! If you listen to her tell it, she's a regular news diva." Bodie's eyes hardened as she looked sharply over her glass. "You're not one of those low-wattage types who think she's hot?"

"I don't like blondes," Leif lied. "For myself, I prefer a woman who looks like a woman." He smiled. "Preferably with red hair." He gestured at his own head. "Less chance to clash, you know."

Bodie's eyebrows rose in her round, expressive face. "Oddly enough, I've got a thing for redheads, too. We'll have to see what we can do about that."

"Ah," Leif said. This was interesting, but not what he'd come here looking for. Time to prod a little. "Forgive me, but I don't think you like Ms. Rush."

"You could say that," Bodie said. "One semester of being her personal servant has just about killed my desire to go into the news business."

"As bad as that?"

"Worse," she assured him. "I had this completely idealistic conception of what journalism was like. You know, the whole Fourth Estate thing."

Leif must have looked puzzled, because she said, "You know, the press as the 'Fourth Estate.' Being European, you must know about the Three Estates of the Realm, right? The Three Estates were the basis of feudal society—the Lords Spiritual, or the Church; the Lords Temporal, or the nobility; and the bourgeoisie, or the common folk."

Actually, Leif *had* learned about that in his history class. He'd forgotten it as soon as it was convenient, as he did much of the information that he learned in school and considered extraneous. Who'd have guessed he'd have a need for that little tidbit? But now he nodded. He remembered enough to get by.

"Well, a couple of hundred years ago, as the press came to have more of an influence on society, journalism was jokingly referred to as a new political force—the Fourth Estate. Then it turned out not to be a joke. By the late twentieth century, newspapers and television had actually helped to unseat one sitting president, and got fairly close to unseating another. Even today, when they get really stuffy and serious, media people like to talk about their responsibility to the public. 'The news sets the agenda,' they say, as if that were a good thing."

"But you began to have your doubts," Leif said.

"To put it mildly," Bodie retorted. "I didn't see anybody in HoloNews carrying the sacred flame. The place is a for-profit business, worse than most of the offices you see in the holos, with all the nastiest parts of Hollywood thrown in."

She shook her head. "I've seen serious stories, mine and everyone else's, pushed aside to make room for coverage of some stupid actor getting caught with his pants down. Other stories I broke got spiked—ignored—because they didn't suit the great Tori Rush's personal agenda. And even when I did get my hands on a hot story, something that was ripe for the headlines, I was just a grunt, the lowest level of employee. I'd do all the work to develop a story, only to see the news diva get the credit. Nobody at the station was ever told how Tori got her hands on the information."

Her full lips twisted. "It was enough to make me sick. Sure knocked all my high ideals about a free press defending democracy right out of my head. A guy named A. J. Liebling had it right: 'A free press is guaranteed only to those who own one.'"

"Tori Rush is that bad?" Leif asked, hoping for some dirt.

"She'd stab you in the back just to get a convenient opening in which to view the time of day," Bodie said. "I'm an intern. I know what goes into the job. I could live with her stealing the credit for all the work I did, and giving me all her work to do on top of it, but then she'd send me out to deal with her dirty laundry and her shopping and her lunches and her bills."

"But if you were handling most of her work and her personal responsibilities, what was *she* doing?"

Bodie glanced around, then her voice became conspiratorial. She wasn't exactly whispering—who could, with that wailing music in the background? But she lowered her

voice and moved her lips closer to Leif's ears. "She's working on setting up her own show."

Leif looked surprised. "But she's the 'fresh new face' on
Once Around the Clock. She's only been there a couple of
years. Is she really such a star that the network would let
her do that?"

"She thinks she's got the demographics," Bodie said.
"There was a time when even the best newsmen—or
-women—needed a decade at the top before they'd get a
shot at their own interview show. They had to stand out
from the rest of the team on the magazine shows just to
get a slot hosting those early-morning extravaganzas that
start at six A.M. On Sundays they had to come up with
probing questions for newsmakers on those panel-interview
shows. But Tori-baby isn't interested in actual work, just
the perks that come with the job. She figures she can push
her status as America's Sweetheart to get what she wants—
money and fame—right now."

Bodie looked truly disgusted. "She spends more time on
the phone with her agent, crafting the latest ultimatum to
the network, than she does checking sources for her stories,
even the stuff she's purloined. Have you noticed that all
the news she's broken lately has been big scandals? Accusations that make headlines, even if they don't stick?
That's 'cause they're easy for her to do. She's got a source
even the network doesn't know about. And those stories
give her a high profile while she does development deals
for her show. You ready for this? She wants to call it *The
Rush Hour*."

Leif shrugged. "Aim high," he said.

"But to get there, she's willing to go really low." Bodie
hesitated for a moment, then shrugged. "I shouldn't really
say this—"

Leif leaned a little closer, but she clammed up again.

"Ah," he said, "this is—what do you call it?—the
teaser?"

Stung, she swallowed the rest of her drink and glared at
him. "Unlike some sources, I come through. The story will
be out soon enough, and I'm quoted in it. Tori, the great

news diva, has hired her own private eyes to dig up dirt for her. How's that for investigative reporting?"

"Detectives?" Leif said in disbelief.

"No shinola, Sherlock. After her agent, the people Tori-babe called most were her professional peepers at I-on Investigations. They were supposed to give her 'background reports.' "

Bodie's lips curled in disgust. "But her highness just prettied them up into news scripts, didn't even bother checking the facts or verifying the stories with multiple sources. I should know. She had me writing up the scripts while she took credit for her 'investigative journalism.' "

"It sounds . . . irresponsible," Leif said, hoping to get more.

"That's the name of the game when you're playing muckraker. Tori wanted and needed a good scandal to make points with the bigwigs. That story about the world-champion pitcher with three wives and three families? That was done based on an I-on report and my scriptwriting. Same thing with that report on the corporate president accused of looting his company's assets."

Leif remembered that one. His father complained that the story had been an unpleasant sandwich—a little bit of truth stuck loosely through thick slices of baloney. The actual dealings the corporate head had approved were perfectly reasonable and legal—but had been cast in an evil light by hysterical reporting, with the usual damaging results for the corporate head. By the time he'd managed to prove his innocence, nobody was listening and the damage to his career and the company had been done.

"Right now Tori's convinced she's latched on to something really good with this story about the Net Force guy killing that gangster," Bodie interrupted Leif's thoughts. "It's got everything—dead innocents, Mafia kingpins, and a great unlikely villain. She's been on the line with her connection at I-on for most of this week, screaming for more dirt."

"And if there is no dirt?" Leif asked.

"Don't be naive," Bodie told him. "Nobody is such a

saint that they haven't done *something*. That Winters guy is history. By the time Tori gets done with the facts, people will be screaming to hang the poor guy."

"Too bad that can't be done to Ms. Rush." Leif had to fight to keep his tone light.

"Oh, she'll get hers," Bodie assured him. "I'm out of the HoloNews internship program as of this morning. You could call this a celebration. I already took care of payback. With a little luck *The Rush Hour* is going to get stuck in traffic, thanks to a long talk I had with Arthur Wellman this afternoon."

"Arthur Wellman?" Leif frowned. "Who's that?"

"Just the founder and chief editor of *Wellman's Fifth Estate*," Bodie told him. "He's great. If I stick with this journalism thing, that's where I want to go to work."

"I know about the Three Estates, and you explained the Fourth Estate," Leif said. "But what is this Fifth Estate?"

Bodie grinned. "Professor Wellman taught journalistic ethics for years at Georgetown University. For years he watched the media become more powerful. You must know the old saying—'Power corrupts.' "

Leif nodded. "The Duke of Wellington said it. 'Power corrupts. Absolute power corrupts absolutely.' "

"The big media outlets—places like HoloNews—come pretty close to absolute power. And they tend to screw around with it. People used to complain that network news was slanted to fit the political views of the reporters. But now you've got lots of big outfits—like the Wolfe Network—where the owner tailors the news to fit his personal agenda or the agendas of his major sponsors. There are news organizations who won't admit that their coverage might have ruined innocent people unless the victims sue successfully. And how many people can afford a long court case? If anybody complains about these abuses, the media giants wrap themselves in the flag and yell about freedom of the press."

Leif nodded. "But I understand there are journalism reviews that discuss such mistakes—"

"Come *on*, Leif," Bodie said. "Those things are put out

by journalism schools. How far are journalism students going to go attacking the companies they hope will hire them? And even then, those things are only read by superbrain researchers. They're like law reviews or medical journals. The only time people hear about anything from those scholarly publications is when their stories are picked up by the popular media."

"Yet the information is on the Net—"

"Sure, if you've got a decent search engine," Bodie shot back. "And enough interest to look. And enough knowledge about the topic in the first place. And a big enough platform to get people to listen to you."

"Wouldn't the networks provide that platform?" Leif said. "I'd expect that a competitor's mistakes would be news."

"That's part of the power problem of the press," Bodie replied. "There seems to be a conspiracy of silence—or maybe it's a gentleman's agreement. Except for a few rare exceptions—usually when a competitor gets sued by another huge corporation and has to shell out big bucks in a court settlement—the networks don't cover those kinds of stories."

Bodie tossed her wild red curls, but her cynical smile turned hopeful. "Professor Wellman intends to change that with *The Fifth Estate*. The magazine is almost out of startup now. It's going to be a regular newsmag, aimed at a general audience, with advertising and everything."

Leif appreciated Bodie's hopes, even shared them, but a little voice in the back of his mind had a nasty question. *And where is the professor going to advertise? Through the very media giants he hopes to embarrass?*

Frankly, Leif wondered if *The Fifth Estate* would be around when Bodie went looking for a job. But he didn't say so. She'd told him a lot more than he'd expected to hear.

Apparently, Bodie thought the time for talking was done, too. "Enough of the whys and wherefores," she said. "Tonight I'm celebrating my escape from HoloNews and Tori Rush. And you're gonna help me, right, rich boy?"

She showed Leif a mouthful of small, sharp teeth in a smile that was downright carnivorous.

So now I know what a man-eater looks like, Leif thought as Bodie dragged him back onto the dance floor.

The things I do to discover the truth. . . .

Next morning Leif got out of bed in slow stages. All his parts and bits seemed to creak as he put weight on them. It was the worst wake-up call he could remember in quite a long time. He was sure of just two things. Bodie Fuhrman took her celebrations seriously, and she had a downright frightening amount of animal vitality.

Leif needed a shower, breakfast, and several cups of strong coffee before he felt up to contacting Megan O'Malley.

She took one look at him over the holo and asked him archly, "Have a nice evening?"

Leif shook his head and regretted it. "You don't want to go there," he said. "Trust me on that. But I did find out a few things."

Quickly he ran through the information Bodie Fuhrman had given him. Megan looked impressed—maybe the evening *had* been worth the price he'd paid.

"I'm going to see if I can find out a little more about I-on Investigations," he said. "Maybe you can take a whack at this magazine, *The Fifth Estate.* If this Wellman guy was a professor at Georgetown University, he might be operating out of D.C."

"I'd rather concentrate on Tori Rush," Megan replied.

"We've got the barest fingernail between the stones in this wall we've been beating our heads against," Leif said. "Do you want to alert this nationally famous newswoman that we know what she's doing? If it's something she wants to deny, all the evidence will disappear."

"And how do you expect me to get at these magazine people?" Megan wanted to know.

"I'm sure you'll figure out a way," Leif said. "Maybe you can be a Net Force Explorer who's worried about the going-over Rush is giving to the captain, searching for a fair venue in the press. That even has the advantage of being the absolute truth." He didn't want Wellman & Co. realizing that Bodie Fuhrman had leaked her knowledge of the story. That was his main reason for having the contact come from Washington rather than New York. Besides his wish to keep his source secret and safe, Bodie might yet be useful.

He ran over a couple of other ideas with Megan, then went for more coffee. Yes, Bodie might indeed still be useful. If he could just survive her. . . .

Megan easily found a Net directory listing for *The Fifth Estate* in the D.C. area. When she called on the holophone, she found herself speaking directly to Professor Arthur Wellman himself. He looked like a Hollywood casting director's idea of what a professor should look like. Wellman was plump, with wispy white hair surrounding a large bald patch. He had a carefully trimmed white mustache, and a thread of smoke rose from the pipe sitting off to one side on his desk.

The professor had a surprisingly young smile. "You're surprised to speak to the head honcho rather than a receptionist?" he said lightly. "This isn't exactly a multinational conglomerate yet. No receptionist so far. And I'm interested in seeing who seeks us out."

"Well, I'm interested in talking to someone who wants to take on the news business," Megan said, honestly enough. "The other magazines my Net search turned up seemed too . . ." she reached for a word.

"Schoolie?" Wellman suggested.

"Pretty close, although I didn't expect a professor to say it," she said. "I'm a Net Force Explorer, and I like to think of myself as a friend of Captain James Winters. Until recently he was pretty anonymous, just a regular guy, but you might have heard of him lately."

Wellman looked a little less amused. His pale blue eyes grew sharper. "Like it or not, he's become a figure in the news."

"More like a target," Megan said. "And the one who

started everybody shooting at him is Tori Rush."

"So you'd like to make her a target of ours?"

I guess Wellman earned his degrees, Megan thought. *He's certainly no dope.*

"Just a question or two. How'd she get all that dirt on Captain Winters? It was all old history, history that made the captain into a hero, not a criminal. Nobody else came up with that stuff, certainly, until she led them there. Who has she got digging?" Megan knew she was pushing her luck but hoped the result would be worth it.

"Has someone approached you?" Wellman seemed almost eager.

Megan shook her head. "I just . . . hear things."

The professor's sharp blue eyes took her in again. "Considering the side you claim to be on, I don't think you heard any such rumor from HoloNews. And I know you didn't hear anything from my operation."

He glanced away from the holo pickup for a moment. "How refreshing. You actually seem to be who you claim you are. Megan O'Malley . . ." Wellman reeled off her address, her age, and several other pieces of information about her.

"How did you—" Megan asked, a little surprised.

Wellman glanced back from the off-pickup display he'd obviously been reading. "*The Fifth Estate* is supposed to be in the journalism business," he said. "You didn't take any extraordinary precautions in contacting us, so it was easy enough—and entirely legal—to trace your call. No different than using Caller ID a generation ago."

His smile was back, perhaps just a tad grim. "You introduced yourself at the beginning of this call. Perhaps you're not aware how much seemingly private information can be accessed from public sources."

"That's not what happened to Captain Winters," Megan shot back. She decided to go for broke. "I heard that Tori Rush hired private eyes to go after him, and they weren't exactly scrupulous about how they did it."

"And I wish I knew where you heard that rumor," Wellman replied.

Megan grinned. "I have to protect my sources—isn't that what all the media types say?"

"And for my part in the game I'd have to answer, 'No comment,'" Wellman said.

"Off the record?" Megan suggested.

Slowly Wellman shook his head. "There's no such thing in the media. And I'm sure you know that."

Megan dropped all pretense of playing reporter. "Professor, I'm trying to help an innocent man who's about to get his life ruined."

"There's a lot of evidence against him, from what I hear."

"Maybe I'll sound like a silly schoolgirl when I tell you this," Megan said. "But I know Captain Winters. Until they find an unimpeachable witness who saw him blow up Stefano Alcista, I'll never believe the charges against him. Everything they've got, as far as I can tell, is circumstantial. I know he didn't do it."

"You believe the evidence is fabricated?" Wellman asked.

"Worse. I suspect that the captain is being intentionally framed. I'm not sure why, but he's being put in a box," Megan responded angrily. "And Tori Rush seems to be the one hammering down the top."

"Interesting." Professor Wellman looked silently at Megan for a long moment.

"Let's consider a hypothetical situation," he said abruptly. "What has been the fastest-growing specialty in the news business in the last fifty years?"

"Overseas reporter?" Megan offered.

"Not a bad answer." The professor nodded. "The global economy has affected the networks, and not necessarily for the better. Foreign audiences have forced broadcasters to give more world news. That's good. But competition from abroad means more competition for national audiences here and abroad. It started more than thirty years ago, when British broadcasters started sending satellite newscasts to the U.S. Now most of Europe and quite a few Pacific Rim nations are competing for the world news market share. It's affected the quality of the news."

"How?" Megan asked.

"After politics, scandal is the easiest sort of news to sell—both inside this country and around the world. Think about the worldwide obsession with the scandals of the British royal family for the past fifty years. Even though they have very little relevancy to most people's lives, we're all interested in them. That news plays everywhere, so you can't escape it." Wellman gave her a lopsided smile. "Most news appeals very differently to different audiences. Local news, for example, rarely plays anywhere out of its home turf. Business news, too, has a limited international audience—investors who can afford to play in the big leagues. But some news hits just about everybody where they live— a juicy scandal is like that. It's got all the lowest common denominators of humanity—sex, money, and murder. Which leads back to my original question: What's the fastest-growing news specialty?"

Megan admitted defeat. "What?"

"Being an expert in front of the cameras. When there's a war, the networks trot out ex-generals to explain the strategy. If there's a financial crisis, economists try to put it in perspective. Lawyers become part of the coverage of big trials. When a serial killer is caught, or some terrible crime is committed, psychologists appear like magic all over the HoloNet."

Professor Wellman shrugged. "Given this influx of specialists into the news—and we're being strictly hypothetical here, remember—we have to ask a question. How long could it be before someone brought in investigative specialists to help—or replace—investigative reporters? Perhaps we are now looking at the results of that very process."

7

Leif sat at the breakfast table, frowning. He'd volunteered to find out more about I-on Investigations. But his Net search had turned up very little—just a scattering of news articles about a new CEO and some expanded business.

Right, Leif thought. *They went into show business.*

His father poured himself a cup of coffee. "You look deep in thought today," Magnus Anderson said.

"And I've got very little to show for it," Leif replied. Then an idea hit him. "Dad, when you went out with Deborah Rockwell, did she ever talk about business?"

"Back to that, are we?" Magnus shrugged. "She tended to keep whatever she was working on under wraps. Why?"

"What do you think she'd say about a newsperson who hired private investigators to dig up information for a story she was working on and then didn't bother to double-check it before broadcasting news based on it?"

"I imagine Deborah would have to doubt the competence of that newsperson," Magnus said slowly. "The networks have staff people—researchers, fact checkers, and so forth—to develop the background for the stories the reporters dig up. But, in the end, it's up to the journalist to get it right—

he or she makes the judgment calls in creating stories. Hiring outside assistance—that doesn't strike me as good judgment for a reporter. Not double-checking such information strikes me as career suicide."

"Well, Tori Rush is in the process of committing it, then," Leif said. "She's apparently working with an outfit called I-on Investigations to trash Captain Winters. I thought it might be a good idea to check those people out—"

"You, and a couple thousand of your Net Force Explorer friends, no doubt," his father said with a laugh.

Leif nodded. "Maybe. The part that's not funny is that my friends think I know what I'm doing. Sometimes I even do—but this time I'm in over my head, and it's frightening. This might be important, Dad. Captain Winters's career, maybe even his freedom, could depend on what we find out. But I don't seem to be getting anywhere on the Net."

"Perhaps that's because you're not a professional investigator," Magnus said gently. "You have some sources that even network research types might envy. But this job seems to require a serious attack. Luckily, I think we can handle it in-house."

Leif knew that his father didn't mean the answer was inside their home. His dad was referring to the company he had founded—Anderson Investment, Multinational. It was a large and very profitable concern, a brokerage house that was an investor's paradise, with investigative resources Leif could never hope to access on his own. Just as he'd planned, his dad had taken the ball and run with it.

Now, Leif thought, *it's just a matter of time until Captain Winters is cleared.*

Two days later Leif visited his father's offices, hoping that his dad had come through, and that all Captain Winters's troubles would be over. Leif was conducted to a conference room, where Magnus Anderson met him at the door. There was an attractive woman seated at the table in the center of the room.

"Anna Westering, this is my son Leif," Magnus said in

introduction. The woman who rose from her seat at the big shiny walnut table looked rather petite beside Magnus Anderson's Viking-chieftain physique. But Leif noticed that she had a firm grip when she shook hands with him—a very firm grip, and some odd calluses.

"Karate, Ms. Westering, or one of the more esoteric martial arts?" he asked.

"How observant you are," she replied with a slight smile. "Karate it is."

Leif shrugged. "Net Force Explorers are expected to learn a bit in the way of self-defense. I've noticed that many of the Marine instructors they bring in have similar ridges of callus on their hands."

Anna Westering cocked her head to the side, then glanced at Magnus. "There's more to your son than meets the eye. There's potential there."

See, Dad? I've always told you that, Leif thought but wisely didn't say.

"Ms. Westering is the company's new head of security," Magnus explained.

Leif glanced at her in surprise. Old Thor Hedvig, the last head of security, recently retired, had been about as big as Leif's father. He'd started out as a driver-bodyguard and had risen through the ranks of the company as Anderson Investments had grown.

"I asked Anna to take a look into I-on Investigations," Magnus Anderson went on.

"Which I did," Anna said. "Of course, we don't use outside agencies for our investigations here at Anderson Investments. We prefer to utilize long-term hires—people who'll know our company and our needs." Anna Westering shrugged. "And who will be far less inclined to talk about anything we don't want talked about. Of course, we do occasionally utilize a few contract operatives to handle out-of-the-ordinary technology, or sometimes urgent circumstances."

Hackers and corporate spies, you mean, Leif thought. Aloud, he asked, "Do you see a problem with agencies like I-on?"

"From my point of view, yes," Westering replied. "I don't object to what they do, of course. I'm in much the same business myself. My problem with outfits like I-on is with security. You can't win an agency's unswerving loyalty, the way you can a corporate employee's. And you can't check an agency out exhaustively, the way you can with a single contract operative. There are too many people tied into an organization like I-on for a real background check to be effective."

"So what is it that they do better than an investigative reporter?"

Anna Westering gave him a half-smile. "Investigative reporters are trained to investigate and to report what they discover in an interesting manner to the public. A good security person, or investigator, investigates and reports, but only to the person paying for the investigation. And the buyer doesn't care about ratings, only about results. Journalistic researchers can investigate the public record, and, if they're good hackers, they might know how to penetrate some more private datafiles. Private detectives—at least the better kind—are aware of more avenues to get information than a typical reporter or researcher. Of course, many of those routes are neither public nor legal, but investigators usually have connections in place to help them get what they need to get the job done."

She spread her hands. "I'll give you an example from a typical HoloNet mystery. How often do you see the detective hero enter the local Net node, claim to be a police officer, and find the name connected with a particular phone number? I assure you, Leif, that particular trick won't work in real life. But there are published databases—national and international reverse directories—that list phone numbers in a searchable form with their associated information. You can use those databases to do a search based on phone number and come up with the name and address of the person who has that phone number. The typical person in the street wouldn't know how to get that information without a bit of research. A trained investigator, whether a reporter or private eye, would not only know, he'd have such a database handy. And that's legal investigation. I leave the picture of the illegal avenues of investigation available to various detectives to your imagination—your father assures me it's a *very* active imagination. I wouldn't want to corrupt such a promising mind."

"So tricks like that are how Tori Rush was able to assemble so much information on the captain in such a short time," Leif said. "It's just basic info-crunching on an exalted scale."

Westering nodded. "Yes. She'd probably apply the same kind of methods used by the low-end private investigative outfits that advertise their services all over the Net for searching out lost friends and loved ones. Given a few sketchy details—full name, date of birth, Social Security number—they can grind through all the public datafiles, state and federal, to find a match. But there's far more and far better data held in private by companies and individuals. Successful investigators know how to tap into that secret sea of information, whether the database holders want them to or not."

Leif couldn't help himself. "And then they spy into people's private lives."

Westering looked at him in silence for a moment. "You're awfully quick to judge, even while you're demanding information from that very same sea." Her eyes challenged him. "Is it so different from what the agents of Net Force do? Or what you do yourself when you need to know something about someone? For the record, I did the same sort of work for Interpol before I went into the private market."

"Perhaps you can tell us what you found this time," Magnus Anderson interjected, trying to head off any argument.

Anna Westering nodded. "The basic information is pretty run-of-the-mill. I-on Investigations started up about seven years ago. It's what's known in the trade as a 'cop shop,' founded by several retiring police detectives." She shrugged. "Happens often enough. Most states require that anyone applying for a private investigator's license should have prior experience in the field. Police detectives are, of course, trained in basic investigative procedure . . . although they may not be up on the latest techniques."

Anna's lips twisted. "Ex-cops would also expect to get a lot of work because of their former employment. That doesn't always happen. It didn't for I-on. The company was frankly floundering until it was taken over by new management."

"I knew they'd been taken over," Leif said. "That much I found in the business datafiles."

Magnus Anderson looked interested. "What sort of people take over a failing detective agency?"

"Foreign money, sir," Anna said.

Leif noticed that the woman showed his father considerably more respect than he got. His dad had probably earned it the hard way—and it was certainly deserved.

"What kind?" Leif asked.

"I haven't succeeded in pinning that down." She frowned. It clearly bothered her that the shell game hadn't yielded to her inquiries. "The new CEO is a Marcus Kovacs. The name is Hungarian, but his background—"

"Is lost in one of the Balkan wars, I'll bet," Magnus Anderson finished for her. "A lot of people have that sort of cloudy past. Some of those clouded pasts are even legitimate."

Westering nodded again, this time more cautiously. "I-on has done considerably more business—and made more profit—since the new management came in. A lot of new blood has been hired—hackers. And they've gotten a certain . . . reputation."

"What kind?" Leif and Magnus Anderson both asked.

Anna Westering shrugged unhappily. "My father had a phrase he used to use as a joke: 'You lie, and I'll swear to it.' Some people say that I-on takes that saying seriously—and that they take it further than that. You lie, and they won't just swear to it, they'll even create the evidence to back up your story."

"She said *what?*" Megan demanded after Leif made his report. They and the rest of the D.C. crew were floating again in Matt Hunter's virtual workspace, sharing information—and attitude, Megan had to admit.

"This is just great," she went on. "We've got newspeople who think they're defending democracy while breaking their own rules, and detectives who succeed by lying and cheating."

" *'Quis custodiet ipso custodes?'* " David Gray quoted.

"If that's something about custodians, I don't want to hear it," Andy Moore cracked.

Matt and Andy had recently saved their school from being blown up by a spy disguised as a custodian. Megan didn't find the reference particularly funny, under the circumstances. She steered the conversation back to the subject at hand.

"It means 'Who will guard the guardians?' " she said.

"More like 'Who will watch those very same watchmen?' " Leif spoke up unexpectedly. "In the original source material, the Latin poet Juvenal was making a joke about keeping wives faithful."

That got a stare from Megan and everybody else in the room.

Leif shrugged. "Just another symptom of an expensive but generally useless education," he said.

"Let's get back to the point," Megan said. "Where does this new information get us?"

"It gets us a bunch of new questions," Matt said.

"Like?" Megan challenged.

"Like," Leif said, "if Tori Rush had I-on Investigations create a case against Captain Winters . . . why did she do it? Why him? What has she got against the captain?"

"*If* she had them do that?" Megan glared at Leif. "What's that supposed to mean? Are you starting to think Captain Winters is guilty of all this crap?"

"I think that either the captain is suffering from the lousiest series of coincidences in all of history, or he's being set up," Leif said flatly. "Going by the 'Motive, Opportunity, and Means' stuff fed to Matt by Agent Dork, what have we got?"

"We have an organization with a rep for creating evidence." Matt held up a finger. "That gives us means, I guess."

"And there were days between the Alcista killing and Net Force I.A. searching the captain's house," Maj Green said. "That has to be a window of opportunity."

"But we still have no motive," Leif said. "The other guys who got put under the microscope had at least done something to catch Tori Rush's interest. The ballplayer had extra wives. The corporate guy was juggling his company's money. All Winters did was go on TV and get sandbagged."

"Maybe this Rush babe is a friend of Jay-Jay Mc-Guffin's," Andy suggested.

"That almost sounds serious," David said in mock amazement.

"I didn't think to ask that," Leif admitted. "Guess I'll have to get back to people and check."

"I'll take another run at *The Fifth Estate,*" Megan said. "If my new friend Professor Wellman can't think of a possible connection between Rush and McGuffin, he's sure to have a lot of people he can check with."

She thought for a second. "I'll also hit him with I-on's reputation. He should know about that if he's doing a story about them being in bed with Tori Rush." Megan shrugged. "Be interesting to see what he's gotten on this Kovacs guy and the people who bought the company." She grinned at Leif. "Maybe we'll see if the media research types manage to beat out A.I.M.'s investigators. It might interest your dad, anyway."

"You're all forgetting something," David Gray pointed out. "That so-called test blast Hangman Hank Steadman's guys discovered in their Net Search."

He looked seriously around at the other kids floating in space. "That happened after Tori Rush first plastered Captain Winters's face around the Net—but before Alcista was blown up."

"Coincidence," Maj tried to bluster. But her voice sounded shaken.

"It's marked with the same chemical tracers as the IA

techs found in the captain's workshop—and in the bomb that killed Alcista." David's voice was inexorable. "That's one hell of a coincidence. In fact, the more I think about it, the more it scares me."

Calm, cold David Gray never gets scared, Megan thought. *At least he never talks about it. Now I'm scared.*

But she could see why this sudden insight would upset him. It upset her.

Ever since she heard about the Alcista bombing, she'd figured it for an organized-crime hit which someone had twisted to attack Captain Winters.

But if the false evidence trail was being planted before the bombing, that meant whoever set out to frame James Winters also blew up Stefano Alcista.

It would take a really sick puppy to commit a murder just to create a news story.

"Net Force I.A. got that bombing report through a Net Search," Matt offered. "What if someone tampered with the date—or even inserted the report after creating a phony crater and bomb?"

"What-if and maybe," Leif grumbled. "This is Net Force we're talking about here. They should be able to detect if anyone was screwing around with those records. We can't just wish evidence away. Otherwise, we're not going to have any solid facts to work with."

We've got one solid fact, Mr. Smart-ass Anderson, Megan told herself. *We know that Captain Winters is innocent.*

At least, she amended, *I do.*

8

After David's liberal dose of cold reality, calling *The Fifth Estate* seemed almost pointless.

But it's all I can think of doing to help the captain, Megan told herself. She sat down at her computer system and gave the orders for a holographic connection. Once again she was quickly connected to the newsmag's professorial publisher.

Professor Wellman didn't seem surprised to see Megan on the other end of the holophone line.

He didn't seem very enthusiastic, either.

"More hypothetical questions, Ms. O'Malley?"

"Just plain, ordinary ones," Megan replied. "Some people I talked with had interesting things to say about I-on Investigations. Seems they have a really creative touch with evidence. It appears like magic to back up whatever stories their clients want to sell."

"Wellman nodded, but his expression still wasn't encouraging. "If so," he said, "they haven't been caught at it yet. Otherwise, their license would have been pulled. That could merely be badmouthing by people on the other side who lost court cases."

So, Megan thought, *he already knows what I told him, but he probably can't prove it.*

"My second question goes more to motive—why someone would try to get James Winters in trouble. Hardly anyone outside of Net Force—and the Explorers—knew the captain before he went on *Washington People.* That's where the interviewer tried that trick question and got the reaction everyone saw on *Once Around the Clock.* The local reporter, Jay-Jay McGuffin, took a lot of grief from Net Force Explorers after the show aired. Kids from all over the country wanted a piece of him."

"You're making a case for young McGuffin to seek revenge against James Winters," Wellman said in his most professorial voice.

"I was wondering if he had a friend higher up in the network," Megan said. "Someone on *Once Around the Clock.*"

"Someone like Tori Rush," Wellman finished for her. Not only did he sound like a teacher, the teacher was clearly disapproving of his student's answer.

"Tori Rush started out in HoloNews local outlets in the western states," Wellman said. "She never worked in Washington, whereas Mr. McGuffin has only worked in the D.C. area. As far as we've been able to ascertain, there is no connection—friendly or otherwise—between the two of them."

"Then where did she get the clip of Winters?" Megan asked in frustration. "She can't scan every episode of every local news show—"

"An interesting question," Wellman responded. "One I haven't been able to find an answer for."

That reminded Megan of the answers Anna Westering hadn't been able to get. "Do you know anything about the foreign investors who bought up I-on Investigations? It seems like a weird investment, picking up a failing cop shop."

"I-on has been remarkably profitable under its new management," Wellman pointed out.

Yeah, Megan thought. *Telling lies for fun and profit.*

That's bound to pay better than catching errant spouses in the act.

"How about the new head honcho?" she asked.

"Ah, the elusive Mr. Kovacs." Wellman allowed himself a slight smile. "There's very little about him on the record—and what records exist are remarkably war-torn. The village where he was supposedly born no longer exists. His school records were wiped out when a cruise missile went off-course. There are some college records for a Marcus Kovacs, but he seems to disappear for years. And he wasn't very forthcoming when we interviewed him."

"*The Fifth Estate* actually went up and asked him questions?" Megan said. "Won't that warn him that a story is coming out about his association with Tori Rush?"

"No," Wellman replied. "He was under the impression he was being profiled by a small business journal."

Megan stared at him. "After all the stuff you said about journalists abusing their power—aren't you doing the same thing?"

"A profile will appear in that journal," Wellman said stiffly. "But we'll be able to use the information as well."

"You did lie to him, though."

"A stratagem." Wellman's pink face went pinker still. "We have to live in the world as it is. Kovacs would have boxed us out the minute he learned we knew he was working for Tori Rush. He'd claim client privilege, and we probably wouldn't even have gotten any general information on his company. This way *The Fifth Estate* got information on I-on and images of Kovacs—he's remarkably camera-shy—and *The Review of Small Business* got a story as well."

"You have pictures of Kovacs?" Megan said.

"A few." Wellman's small smile appeared again. "He told our photographer he was a very busy man."

"Could I see one?" Megan requested.

Know your enemy, she thought.

Wellman dug around on his desk and came up with a sheaf of flatcopy images. "This is the one we're considering for our story," he said, holding up one of the pictures.

Marcus Kovacs was a remarkably hairy man. A thick,

full beard covered his jaw, meeting unfashionably long hair that brushed his collar. Both his beard and his mane of hair were dark, flecked with gray.

"He looks more like a poet than a private eye," Megan said. "Much less the head of a company."

Out of sight of the pickup, her hands danced on her computer's keyboard, ordering an image capture from the holographic display. Now she'd have this picture of Kovacs, as well.

Wellman ran through a sequence of images. Apparently deep in thought over the answer to one of the interviewer's questions, Kovacs ran a hand through his leonine mane, revealing that at least one ear hid behind all that hair. The next picture his hand was down, moving toward the camera. The third picture just showed the palm of his hand.

"That was the end of our photo session," Wellman said dryly. "It seems Mr. Kovacs has the temperament of a poet, as well. His background, however, seems to be in finance. That's what he told our interviewer. He had been hired by the takeover group to spruce up the company, probably with the idea of reselling it. But he proved himself to be a more than competent manager, not merely juggling the books, but actually making tremendous profits where none had previously been made."

While pushing the company's mission into the gutter of falsifying evidence, Megan thought.

"Two final questions," she said. "When is your story coming out . . . and why are you telling me all of this?"

"You have a most refreshing directness, Ms. O'Malley—and a touching innocence, if I may say so." Professor Wellman removed his glasses, cleaning them with a small piece of cloth. But out from behind the lenses, his eyes seemed even sharper as he looked at her.

"My dear young lady, you're a source on a high-profile story," Wellman said. "At some point, as this story develops, *The Fifth Estate* may turn to you for a reaction from one of Captain Winters's protégés. We've already tried contacting the captain directly. He's strictly incommunicado at the moment.

"Anyway, when the time comes for us to seek information, I hope you'll remember that we were generous in answering your questions. *Quid pro quo,* you see."

The only thing I see is that I'm bumping into a lot of Latin on this case, Megan thought grimly. *And everything else is Greek to me.*

"In answer to your first question, the Rush/I-on story is scheduled to come out in two weeks." Wellman frowned. "Because we cover the media, we have to make sure all of our facts are absolutely true before we publish. I think we'll end up regretting that policy. Events are moving faster than I'd wish. Instead of exposing the story, we may end up as a footnote in a much larger media frenzy."

"Meaning?" Megan said, almost afraid to hear his answer.

Wellman tried to keep his tone gentle, but his words hit Megan like brutal blows. "Meaning our voice will just be lost in the stampede, once Captain Winters is indicted for Stefano Alcista's murder."

Leif took a call from Megan O'Malley and got a storm of worried anger as well as a few nuggets of information.

"Hey, what does a retired journalism professor know about the law?" he said, trying to make her feel better. But he had to admit that his words sounded hollow even in his own ears.

About an hour later Leif received a virtmail notice for another special meeting of the Net Force Explorers for the next day. Coming after Megan's call, this looked ominous.

"Maybe that professor *does* know something," Leif muttered grimly. "They're probably getting us together now to soften the blow when Steadman's report comes out." Now he wished that no one had told him the nickname attached to the head of Net Force Internal Affairs. "Hangman Hank" didn't sound like a joke anymore.

Leif barely picked at his dinner that evening.

"Are you feeling all right?" his mother asked.

"Just things on my mind," Leif replied. Tonight was the night *Once Around the Clock* came on. Maybe today Captain Winters—and all the Net Force Explorers—would be lucky. Maybe Tori Rush would find a new target.

Of course, that dream was doomed from the start. Tori Rush was right up there in the first half of the show, trumpeting the damning findings of the as-yet-unreleased Net Force Internal Affairs report.

What a surprise that it should be leaked to her, Leif thought coldly. *I wonder if newsdiva Tori got the report through her own connections, or did I-on hack it out of the Net Force computers in time for her to get it on this evening's broadcast?*

If the rogue investigators had hacked the report, that left them open to criminal charges. That illegal act would make a nice lead-off to the revelation that Tori—the supposedly pure and untarnished journalist—was hiring detectives to do her dirty work for her. It might even splash all over the media with a newsworthy bang.

The only problem was, it wouldn't do a single thing to get James Winters off the hook. As Matt Hunter had heard from Agent Dorpff, I.A. had assembled a damaging, if circumstantial, case against Captain Winters. These days the whole world knew Winters had a motive for killing Stefano the Bull. He apparently had the opportunity—and no alibi. The tagging chemicals from the bomb that destroyed Alcista's car and its occupant had also been discovered in the captain's garage workshop.

But the worst part was the practice bomb. For one thing, it made Winters look like a cold-blooded killer, carefully tailoring the blast to get the best—or was that the worst?—out of it. As David had pointed out, the very existence of a test blast before Alcista's murder and before the story was all over the national media made it unlikely that Winters was being framed for murder after the fact by someone who'd seen the various broadcasts. So it wouldn't help to accuse Tori Rush of hiring detectives who provided evidence on demand.

Unless, Leif thought, the person who framed Winters was also the person who killed Alcista. Call him or her X, the mystery murderer. Who could it be? A tremendously wily organized-crime hit person? A former spy turned assassin? That led nowhere, or rather in too many directions at once. Try motive instead—why would someone do what had been done?

Had the captain been cold-bloodedly chosen as a convenient scapegoat by the real murderer? That could work. Suppose one of Alcista's former associates didn't want him pushing back into the business? It would be quite convenient to hand over James Winters to take the blame. It might even be satisfying. Winters had undoubtedly busted a number of mob types in his career. Maybe one of them set him up as payback.

It didn't even have to be a professional hit, Leif realized. There were probably lots of other people out there who hadn't been delighted to see Steve the Bull loose on the streets again. After all, the guy prided himself on breaking legs and killing people. Anyone who'd survived his business methods—or vengeful family members and friends of those who hadn't—might want to take out Alcista, for obvious reasons. And once Winters's furious face appeared on Washington's holo displays courtesy of Jay-Jay McGuffin—anyone could have chosen him as a patsy.

If someone who planned to kill Alcista had watched Jay-Jay's interview, they'd have had James Winters delivered to them as a scapegoat, just like the answer to a prayer.

Leif tightened his grip on the arms of his chair, trying to keep his confused thoughts from making his head whirl any faster.

Time to stop this, he told himself. *These ideas are sounding more and more like plot lines from the afternoon holosoaps.* None of them offered an avenue of investigation to clear the captain.

Vendettas, personal or business-related, might be colorful but didn't help narrow down the range of possible murderers here. If anything, the idea added to the candidates. Leif doubted that he or even all his Explorer friends could check out such a mob of suspects. A job like that would require the talents and resources of a national law-enforcement agency dedicated to finding the killer.

Like Net Force, Leif thought bitterly. *Unfortunately, Net Force already has a handy-dandy suspect—Captain James Winters.*

Matt flashed in early for the special Net Force Explorers meeting. He wanted to be close to the stage tonight, even though the reason for the evening's assembly wasn't exactly a surprise anymore.

As he blinked into the virtual hall, he was surprised to see how many people had been inspired with the same idea. Matt was faced with a good-sized horde when he arrived. And the horde wasn't in a good mood. Kids were actually snarling because the usually polite and easygoing attendees were anything but tonight.

"Nice group," Andy Moore commented as he finally reached the D.C. bunch. His hair was even wilder than ever after a near-scuffle on the way to join Matt, Leif, Megan, and the others.

"When you're happy, you want to share it," Leif said bitterly. "I wonder who they have on hand to sugarcoat all this wonderful news."

"I hope it's not Steadman," David Gray muttered. "It's a good thing this meeting's virtual. If Steadman turns up, I think the kids will storm the stage."

That's what this whole setup feels like, Matt suddenly

realized. *A lynch mob. Except it's Captain Winters getting lynched, and we can't seem to do anything about it.*

By the time the meeting was supposed to start, just about every present Explorer—and maybe some past ones—had appeared in the room, waiting to hear the official explanation. Matt felt a bit claustrophobic. Even though the room's walls were elastic, the crowd was determined to get as close as possible to the podium. Kids shoved forward, banging into people with their elbows as they unconsciously squeezed closer, and getting banged in return until they could barely move their arms. Matt found himself standing uncomfortably close to the girl in front of him.

It's just a sim, he kept reminding himself. *Just a sim.* Even so, he found himself bothered by Andy Moore's breath steaming against his ear.

Just when full-blown claustrophobia was about to roll through him, Matt felt a faint beeping from his wristwatch. *Meeting time,* he thought with relief. *At least now we'll know what's going on.*

But the virtual stage didn't pop into existence. No one declared the meeting open. Neither Agent Dorpff nor whoever would join him in explaining the next move in the Winters case put in an appearance. A few minutes passed.

Then the sullen silence that had filled the room in expectation of the meeting time vanished in a confused outcry of pure fury. If the crowd had been unhappy a moment before, it was downright ugly now.

"What the hell is going on?" an especially piercing voice cut through the wall of noise. "This is like incompetent city. All of a sudden Net Force can't keep its own information in its computers. And now they can't even start a meeting on time!"

The noise cut off when the virtual stage at last began to appear. But the subdued roar came back, lower and more ominous, when the kids saw only Len Dorpff standing before them. Still, nobody was yelling—yet. The sound was more like a low growl. It made the hairs on the back of Matt's neck stand up in some sort of caveman reaction.

Dorpff stepped forward like a man walking into an icy

rain. "Welcome to this special meeting of the Net Force Explorers," he said, using the traditional opening for a meeting. It only seemed to emphasize that Captain Winters wasn't there.

"I apologize for holding things up. It can't have been comfortable, but it couldn't be helped, either. Jay Gridley was supposed to be here, to help explain this, ah—"

"Situation," a voice sneered from somewhere in the crowd.

Dorpff ignored the heckler, plunging right ahead. "Unfortunately, he's had to attend a press conference and hasn't been able to get free—"

"So we could have found out more about what's going on if we'd stayed home and watched HoloNews," a female voice said.

Matt recognized the person behind that interruption. It was Megan O'Malley, and she was speaking loud enough to be heard over half the virtual room.

"Again, I regret the change of plans, the delay, everything," Dorpff said.

I bet he especially regrets having to be out there all on his lonesome, Matt thought.

But Dorpff continued doggedly onward. "So it looks like it's up to me alone to try and explain things."

"So get on with it," somebody called out from the crowd. "Is that stuff we saw on *Once Around the Clock* last night a lying load of crap from the actual report, or just a lying load of crap the network made up?"

"The unauthorized announcement of Captain Steadman's findings was unfortunate and, I'm sure, distressing." Dorpff was picking his words with the greatest care, but Matt could see the young agent's effort wasn't going to work.

"Yes or no?" The words were loud enough to make the people closest to the speaker wince. "Was Tori Rush's report from the real deal, or did Steadman come up with something different?"

Dorpff was being pushed into a corner. He looked like a trapped rodent up there on the podium as he stood in silence, unwilling to answer. Then he finally responded to the shouted demand. "The news broadcast was only a summary of the report, presented in the most excessive language." The young agent hesitated. "But, in general, yes, it did present the conclusions of the Internal Affairs investigation."

A low, hollow moan greeted this announcement, as if every person in the room had been simultaneously stabbed. Matt recognized the feeling, even though he thought he'd been prepared to hear the bad news.

A second later, however, the room sounded as if the furies of hell had been released.

"Steadman must have a circuit cracked if he thinks he can just sell the captain down the river!" somebody yelled.

"Creep's been so busy playing his little rat-scragging games, he can't be straight with anyone," another voice joined in.

"He'll learn this time," yet another voice threatened. "After he has a couple of thousand people red-line angry with him."

"Yeah! Let's flame Steadman!"

Other voices took up that cry.

Dorpff could see that the meeting was sliding out of his control. "You can't be serious!" he cried. "That's against the law."

"So's destroying an honest man. You're getting rid of Winters. So who's gonna stop us?" another Explorer wanted to know. "You gonna arrest us all?"

The room echoed with the shouts of angry young people.

"From the sounds of this, the guy will be lucky if he doesn't get his house burned down." Andy thought he was being funny, but Matt could hear the deadly promise in the kids' threats. If some of these guys went ahead with what they were saying, Steadman would be lucky to have a computer left—and any electronic stuff near it. The situation in this room was not good, definitely not good.

Dorpff was getting angry now. "You're talking about breaking a set of laws that Net Force takes very seriously," he said. "Don't think that shouting from the crowd will cover you. If anything happens, Captain Steadman will be reviewing the computer record of this meeting. His techs will track you down if it takes months!"

It was exactly the worst thing to say.

"Then they'll be pretty busy," one of the furious kids shot back, "because we all want to give Hangman Hank a taste of his own medicine!" Murmured agreement shot through the crowd.

Agent Dorpff stared around the room like a stag at bay . . . or like a man watching his career go down the toilet.

Then a truly surprising voice roared out, "Is this what Captain Winters taught you? Taught *us?*"

Matt twisted his head in astonishment. That was David Gray!

David poured it on. "The two biggest things I learned from the captain were his respect for people—and his respect for the law. That's how I know he's innocent."

He glared around at the crowd. "I don't know what *you* people learned, screaming at our liaison agent, planning to attack a Net Force Officer—and through the *Net,* at that!"

His words must have been getting through, because the noise level from the mob was dying down.

David went on in a slightly milder voice. "I don't even see how doing what you were talking about would help the captain. And even if it did, even if it proved Captain Winters innocent, how would he feel, knowing you'd broken the law to do it?"

Now the other Net Force Explorers were silent, looking downright embarrassed.

"The captain wouldn't want us to act like this—so let's honor him here by listening to what Agent Dorpff has to say."

Dorpff spoke up. "I can understand that feelings run high. Certainly, I don't want to believe—" He broke off, as if afraid to stir up those feelings again. "But the proof is hard to contest."

"How would we know?" a bitter voice asked. "All the Net Force Explorers have to go on is a summary of what the I.A. people found—as reported by a scandal-seeking news reporter. Nobody is telling us what's in the report."

"I've seen the report—" Dorpff began, then stopped again. "I can't ask Internal Affairs to release the report to everyone. Nor can we discuss the report in full. Neither would be fair to Captain Winters. But I think, with Winters's permission and the cooperation of Internal Affairs, someone might explain some of the more important specifics to a representative of the Net Force Explorers."

The young agent ran an eye over the crowd. Then he stopped, pointing . . . at Matt.

"I know Captain Winters put a lot of trust in Matt Hunter," Dorpff said. "He lives in the D.C. area, which should make arranging such a meeting easier."

Only then did he seem to realize the enormity of what he'd promised. "Provided I can get Captain Steadman to agree."

Matt walked the corridors of the Net Force operations center, following a different route than he usually took. But then, his destination wasn't Captain Winters's office—or, as things seemed now, his former office.

No, this afternoon Matt was heading for the lair of Hangman Hank Steadman.

The offices of Internal Affairs weren't all that different from the other Net Force agents' offices that Matt had visited.

What were you expecting? Matt asked himself. *Thumbscrews? A torture rack?*

Except for the fact that it didn't have an outside view or a virtual window, Steadman's office could have been a twin of any of them.

Hangman Hank jerked up from his desk, his face twisted in a sneer.

"I can't believe I agreed to this," he growled, his voice contemptuous. "I can't believe Dorpff even suggested it. Right out of the academy, and he can't handle a bunch of kids—caving in to them."

"Agent Dorpff headed off what could have been a nasty wave of virtual and public sabotage." *With a big assist from David,* Matt added silently. "I'm sure you heard about what happened to that local reporter, Jay-Jay McGuffin."

"It would be different, trying that nonsense against a Net Force agent." Steadman glanced at Matt and smiled. It wasn't a pleasant expression. "And after you see some of what we've assembled, you might not be so gung-ho on Winters anymore."

He introduced Matt to a member of his technical staff, who led them immediately to a well-equipped lab.

"Show him the spectrographic analysis of the blast debris," Steadman ordered.

One of the technicians hustled over to a computer console.

Looks like Steadman runs a tight ship, Matt thought. *Maybe a little too tight.*

A couple of quick commands, and a holographic display sprang into existence. It showed several bands of light. "The top image is a spectrograph of the debris from the remains of Stefano Alcista's car. It shows the chemical composition of the explosive that gave Steve the Bull such a blast."

Steadman pointed to a smeared set of bands. "These here represent the trace agents used to tag the particular batch of Semtec, which was manufactured shortly after James Winters's wife was killed."

Another order, and a similar display appeared below the first.

"This is a spectrograph of the residue we found in Winters's workshop."

Matt had never considered himself a science superbrain, but even he could spot the same smear of light.

"The same tagging agents," Steadman said.

At his order, a third spectrograph appeared. "This is from the blast crater in the next township from Winters's house," Steadman announced silkily. "Note—"

"I can see," Matt said tersely.

"Shall we move on to your friend's so-called alibi?" Hangman Hank asked.

"Captain Winters said he was contacted by a snitch—" Matt began.

"Well, if he was, it happened telepathically," Steadman interjected sarcastically. "Call up the records," he ordered his technicians. "Here's the circuitry usage report from the local phone company. No calls directed to the circuitry node including Winters's office phone. And just in case you ask, no calls to his wallet-phone, either."

Another set of numbers came up. Steadman pointed. "Here's the Net Force phone log, security sealed in our own computers. Do you see any incoming phone activity recorded for the captain's office?"

"One thing hanging around Net Force has taught me is that records can be altered—even deleted," Matt said stubbornly.

"Yeah," Steadman replied with a sneer. "And some skell could steal the Declaration of Independence—just about as easily. I'll grant that it's possible to get in and mess with the phone company. But we're talking Net Force security on our phone logs. If someone could infiltrate our systems like that, I'd hire them immediately as a specialist agent."

He laughed and gave another set of orders. "Here's the clincher. We found these partial prints on some of the debris from the crater in the next township." He paused for a second. "Winters's practice bomb."

"You can't—" Matt began.

"I *can*," Steadman interrupted. "And here's why."

The image of a few twisted bits of metal and plastic appeared. A second later faint designs popped into view, loops and whorls—bits of fingerprints.

"This is a facsimile of James Winters's fingerprints from his government records." The explanation wasn't really necessary. The captain's name was right at the top of the form.

"Now, check this out." Steadman couldn't keep the smugness out of his voice.

The partial prints on the bomb debris suddenly turned bright red. They moved from their positions, rotating around in midair to align with the prints on Winters's records. The fragmentary prints came to rest on the facsimiles. There was no doubt of a match.

"Myself, I'd say that was the most damning aspect of the case," Steadman said.

"But people have known how to lift prints and transfer them for more than thirty years," Matt argued desperately.

"And who'd have done the dirty deed? Evil agents from the twelfth dimension?" Steadman really didn't like anyone questioning his findings.

"Anyone with the capability to pull off a decent black-bag job," Matt retorted. "Not that it needed much in the way of criminal genius to break into Captain Winters's garage. After all, he spends—or spent—most of his time here in his office."

"Except for the afternoon Stefano Alcista was murdered," Steadman pointed out.

Matt forced his voice to remain calm. "You've created quite a case, but it seems to ignore one fact."

"Which is?"

"James Winters is a Net Force agent. But according to you, in carrying out this murder, he made a series of mistakes that even the rawest amateur could have avoided. For instance: If you're going to blow someone up, why build the bomb in your own house and test it nearby where somebody's sure to notice?"

Steadman shrugged. "It's probably the most private workspace Winters could find on short notice."

"Oh, that's right. Winters had to rush everything. Except you've got him planning this caper for four years. That's when he'd have had to get hold of the Semtec, when his wife was killed, isn't it?"

Steadman only frowned.

"More important, Winters has no alibi. Think about it— he's a Net Force agent about to commit a felony. You'd think he'd be able to phony up some sort of record to insert in the computers to put him in the clear."

"Maybe he ran out of time," Steadman suggested.

"He had days before your investigation even started," Matt pointed out. "You'd think taking care of a detail like that would be on his mind in the days afterward, if not beforehand."

"He could have been nervous about tripping alarms if he planted evidence. Why call attention to himself?"

"Yeah, that sure worked out like a charm," Matt said sarcastically. "At least for your case. To me, the captain's insistence that there was a call sounds like the testimony of an innocent man—"

"Who happened to leave his fingerprints all over a practice bomb," Steadman cut Matt off.

"Exactly!" Matt nodded. "Captain Winters would have known he'd need to use rubber gloves while building the bombs for the trial run and the final one. He's a trained investigator. He'd know how much information the lab people can pull of an exploded bomb. And when the first bomb didn't turn out right, would he really have left all those pieces for your people to find? For all we know, they could have been planted—"

"*We* know the bomb exploded there." Steadman's gesture took in his assistants. "That blast brought a tree down. We needed a crane to shift it—and we found traces under the trunk." He leaned his face into Matt's. "The blast was real, the traces are real, the prints are real."

He stepped back, obviously attempting to look reasonable. "I know you look up to this guy. But obviously he made mistakes. Maybe when you decide you're bigger than the law, that's just unavoidable."

Matt clamped his jaw shut. *Well,* he thought, *if anybody should know . . .*

10

The virtmail message hung in holographic projection over Leif's computer system. It was just a Net address, with a typed message: "Meet, eight-thirty."

Leif spent a long moment looking at the glowing letters, but they didn't tell him anything new—like who had sent the anonymous message. He could start hacking to try and track down where the message originated, but he doubted he'd get the job done before the time set for the meeting.

Could it have something to do with his attempts to clear Captain Winters? Maybe it would turn out to be a shadowy figure, like that guy who broke the Watergate scandal. What did he call himself? Deep Voice? No, Deep Throat.

But should he go? It might be the faceless enemy who was trying to engineer the captain's doom. . . .

Leif shook his head in disgust. He must be getting a little nuts on this case if he was thinking that way.

Of course he was going to keep the meeting! He had to find out who was behind the message—even if it was only a dumb joke.

A few steps took Leif to his computer-link couch. He sank back into the comfortable padding, although his muscles were a little tense. That always happened when he prepared to link into the Net these days. Leif had suffered trauma to the nerves around the circuitry implanted in his head. Whenever he synched in to the circuits in the chair, he could expect some measure of agony.

Leif flinched through the pain and mental static that now marked his transition to the Net, and opened his eyes to his virtual workspace. He sat on a New Danish Modern sofa in a wooden-walled room. Through a large window he could see a pale blue sky towering over green fields.

But he wasn't interested in the virtual view. Leif got up and turned to the wall behind him, facing a complicated set of shelves. In another house it might have been called a curio cabinet. But the most curious thing about it was that it covered the whole wall, floor to ceiling, and was completely filled with icons.

Leif could have directed his implant circuitry to take him directly to the meeting site. But he thought it might be better to go armed with a few programs. He picked up a small figurine that looked like a lightning bolt—the program icon for communications protocols. He picked up another, which looked like a man shrouded in a hooded cloak. And after a second's thought he reached for yet another figure which looked like a particularly ugly Chinese demon.

It didn't come free when he touched it. Instead, an entire section of shelving swung out—a secret panel, revealing another set of shelves hidden in the wall. The icons in here represented programs which Leif didn't want borrowed, lost . . . or, in some cases, found.

He hesitated again over the shelf he considered his arsenal and finally took a program icon that looked like a small knife.

Closing the outer shelf, he placed the knife program in his pocket and stood with the other two icons in each hand. Leif held out the lightning bolt and thought of the Net address he'd been given.

An instant later he was flying through a neon paradise— or nightmare, depending on your point of view. Virtual constructs in eye-searing colors competed to put on the best

show in cyberspace. It was part funhouse, part kaleido-
scope. And no matter how much some people might complain, it was an unavoidable part of life here and now.

He flew on, leaving the more heavily trafficked sections
of the Net, zooming off to what he considered the "suburbs"—sites put up by lesser companies, or constructs
which allowed even smaller businesses or individuals to
maintain a Net presence. Several hacker acquaintances of
Leif's operated out of locations like that, moving through
a succession of cheap, anonymous virtual offices.

Could one of them have shifted his base? Leif tried to
remember his most recent credit charges. If a professional
hacker had information, it wouldn't come cheap. He'd hate
to redline his credit accounts. It would bring unwelcome
questions from his parents.

But Leif continued on, entering the bleak outskirts of the
Net. Nobody bothered with eye candy out here. The constructs were all the same: low, plain, utilitarian warehouse-
like structures, marching off to the virtual horizon like chips
on a circuit board—or mausoleums in a cemetery. This was
deep storage, the home of dead—or at least deeply archived—data.

Leif knew some people who hacked into this inactive
memory, erasing hopefully worthless records to create virtual party rooms, or secret rendezvous sites . . . or places to
mousetrap people who poked their noses into the wrong
secrets.

This was like entering the virtual equivalent of a dark
alley. And, while there were all sorts of safeguards in place
to keep people from getting hurt in veeyar, Leif was living—and hurting—proof that there were a few people who
could program around some of those blocks.

Leif looked at the program icon in his other hand and
activated it. The hacker he'd bought it from had described
it as the computer version of a shroud of invisibility. Lots
of people surfed the Net in proxies, false semblances to
hide their true identities. This program took that idea further, turning Leif into the little man who wasn't there,
blanking out all indications of his presence. He'd tried it

out a couple of times at parties and such, and it seemed to work well enough.

This time it would be useful rather than amusing. He wanted to see who was waiting for him before they saw him. And he wanted to know what this mystery person had up his or her virtual sleeve.

There was the address. Leif spiraled down to settle on the roof—and pass through it.

The interior was apparently unused, a big, echoing space about the size of the virtual hall that housed Net Force Explorer meetings. But there was only one person in sight, a pretty girl with brown hair and hazel eyes. Megan O'Malley.

Leif cut his invisibility shield and dug out the knife icon. That was a little item guaranteed to mess up Net programming. Leif hoped it would deactivate any booby traps—and, if necessary, put a little hurt on anyone who might try to attack him.

"I sure hope you're the one who called me here," he told Megan. "Otherwise, we both might be in trouble."

Megan nearly jumped out of her virtual skin at his sudden appearance.

"Did you have to do that?" she snapped. Then, after a deep breath, she said, "You can put away whatever you've got in your other hand. I sent the message."

Leif relaxed slightly. "Nice place you've got here."

"I . . . found it not too long ago," Megan said. "Apparently it was set up for storage but never used." She hesitated for a second. "I thought it would be good for a private talk."

"About?"

"What do you think? The weather?" she flared again, then shook her head. "We've seen how the official world is completely willing to shaft Captain Winters. And the people who want to help him . . . well, they're either too bent on revenge to do anything useful, or they're like Matt Hunter."

"A little too goody-goody for their own good sometimes?" Leif asked.

"He means well, but it's like that petition thing he did.

Really nice, but not terribly effective. He won't go far enough."

"And then he gets co-opted by the powers that be," Leif went on. "If you can consider Agent Dork a power."

Megan nodded grimly. "Matt'll try very hard, but he'll play strictly by the rules. And he'll probably break his heart trying to disprove a very cleverly constructed frame job."

"Yeah. Don't get me wrong," Leif said. "I admire Matt's straight-arrow approach. It gets him pretty far a lot of the time."

"But it's not going to work in this case," Megan insisted. "So it's up to us."

"To do what?"

She leaned close to Leif. "To do whatever has to be done. It's not as though we never did it before. And we didn't even have as good a reason then."

"We also nearly got thrown out of the Net Force Explorers for that excess of . . . initiative," Leif pointed out.

Megan gave him a look. "Yeah. And that's really worried you, considering some of the stuff you've pulled since. You're not about to let some idiot rules get in your way." Her face twisted. "I keep wondering how you got all that information about HoloNews and Tori Rush. Probably charmed it out of some airhead intern. What did it take? A few dances? A couple of drinks? What else?"

Leif could feel the color rising on his face. Sometimes Megan could be downright uncanny. Or had she somehow been checking up on him? Either way, she was giving him a great case of the guilts. Megan had to know he was attracted to her. Was she using that in proposing this partnership?

He took a deep breath. "Okay, so sometimes well-meaning people can cross the line for something they believe in. Going by that reasoning, why couldn't Winters break the rules and kill off Alcista?"

Megan looked as if he'd slapped her in the face. "If that's that way you feel—" she began.

"That's not the way I feel," Leif spoke over her words. "I *bend* rules, skate on thin ice, push my luck—but I know there's such a thing as right and wrong. And in my own way I try not to go over the line, to stay on the side of right. Well, James Winters is one of the rightest people I know." He took a deep breath. "I absolutely know he's innocent. If he wanted Alcista out of the way, he'd try to do it through the court system, not with Semtec. Of course I'll help you. From the looks of things, we'll have to push the envelope further than guys like Matt or David would be willing to go."

Leif stabbed a finger at Megan. "But I hope we both learned a few useful things in our last little adventure. We've got to be straight with each other. This isn't a job for the Lone Ranger here. The person behind this is a killer, and one willing to frame an innocent man in the process. We could be in real danger if we aren't careful. We have to keep in touch. And we back each other up—information-wise, and physically, if necessary."

Megan looked mutinous, but she nodded.

"Fine," Leif said. "Now, you tell me what you've been holding back, and I'll do the same."

Matt paced back and forth across his room, swinging close to his computer system, then turning away again. He'd done his best to destroy the Internal Affairs case against Captain Winters, but it was like pounding his head against a brick wall. He could bring up objections and contradictions, but it was all vaporware compared to the solid evidence and supposed facts Steadman had assembled.

Yes, someone could have broken into the captain's garage and planted traces of plastic explosive on his workbench. A very competent hacker might get into the Net Force computers and mess around with the phone logs. Someone even could have gotten hold of James Winters's fingerprints, lifted them, and put them on the fragments of the practice bomb. Admit the means existed for one bit of black-bag work, and you could allow them all. But if you couldn't come up with evidence to prove those activities took place, all you had was a theory. Hot air.

A smart lawyer might use that hot air to confuse the issue

in court. Matt remembered a pretty infamous Hollywood murder where an old flatfilm star–former athlete had gotten out from under a murder charge that way. But his career— and his life—were ruined ever after.

Matt couldn't wish that on Captain Winters.

There has to be some way to poke a hole in the I.A. case, he told himself. *Where can we begin?* Could they canvass the captain's neighborhood, asking if there had been any suspicious characters hanging around during—what? The past month?

Maybe they should take aim at that so-called practice bomb. Hit anyone who lived near the blast site to find out if they'd heard the explosion and if they remembered anything useful. . . .

Matt scowled. Weeks had gone by. Would people remember the details after that much time? And even if they did, which he doubted, would potential witnesses trust their hazy memories? Or would they simply accept what the media had already told them and repeat it?

Running his fingers through his hair until it stood up like some horrible modern sculpture, Matt continued pacing back and forth. Maybe they should cut right back to the beginning and find someone else with a motive, both for the murder and for the frame-up.

Tori Rush still led the pack for smearing Winters. She wanted a big, fat, juicy scandal. Attacking the honesty and integrity of Net Force would ensure her a lot of attention, maybe even a promotion. But still—to accuse an innocent man of killing someone just to get a network show . . . Matt had a hard time accepting that as a motive for murder.

Could there be a personal motive in the mix? Someone who hated James Winters for some reason? Hated him enough to kill to frame him? It was possible, of course. Finding out if somebody fit that mold would likely mean getting hold of Net Force records to find out who the captain had put away. Neither Steadman nor Agent Dorpff was likely to share that information.

And, as for hacking it out, well, it was illegal, though he knew some Net Force Explorers with the expertise to do it.

Matt jammed his hands into his pockets. It was way illegal. It would probably get someone caught and sent to jail. He couldn't be responsible for that.

On the surface of things it seemed as if there was only one person who was angry enough at the captain to try framing him for murder. Unfortunately, Stefano Alcista didn't seem the kind for subtle vengeance—and he really wasn't the type to blow himself up.

Unless . . . maybe the mob boss faked his death! It would give Steve the Bull a chance to retire while sticking it to the man who'd put him in prison. After all, Alcista had been ready to blow Winters up. Why not ruin his life instead of taking it?

It didn't even have to be a faked death, Matt thought. *We should go after Alcista's medical records. Suppose the guy was sick, didn't have long to live . . .*

He shook his head to clear it of such ridiculous thoughts. That level of brilliant deduction usually turned up at the end of really lame detective shows.

I might as well blame it on the saucer people, trying to discredit the captain because he'd seen a UFO.

What he needed—what everyone on Winters's side needed—was some solid proof that Winters was never near Alcista's car when Steadman and company said he was.

Matt went back over Captain Winters's story. He'd gotten a call from an old informant, requesting a face-to-face. How to prove that? Tackle the informant? But the call didn't necessarily have to come from the real informant. It could have been a computer-generated lure, designed to get Winters away from his office for the crucial time period.

In that case, if the files were right, the captain would have been standing on the corner of G Street and Wilson Avenue waiting for his snitch to arrive. Maybe he could find some way to prove that?

For a second, Matt had a disheartening image of himself standing on the corner, showing Winters's picture to passersby and asking if they remembered seeing him on the corner two weeks ago.

Then inspiration struck. There might actually be a witness with perfect memory—and the ability to prove that the captain was where he said he was. An unshakable witness whose testimony would have true mechanical precision. Wilson and G was a downtown location, and a lot of the buildings around there were protected, at least in part, by security cameras. In the old days of videotape the recording medium might have been changed by now. But digital cameras deposited their images directly into computer memory. Maybe, just maybe, somewhere in a computer downtown, there was an archived image of an annoyed Captain Winters cooling his heels with a nice, convenient time and date stamp on it.

Of course, hacking into those computers would be considered somewhat illegal. . . .

Matt turned to his computer and began snapping orders before he lost his nerve. Somehow, this didn't seem quite as bad as trying to get into the secure files of Net Force.

Besides, Matt told himself, *you can't just hang back and do nothing because of a few stupid rules if you can do something that might really help. . . .*

After an all-nighter on the Net, Matt Hunter sprawled in his computer-link couch, feeling more dead than alive. Carrying bricks on a construction site would probably be more physically demanding. But while his body had lain here, getting the occasional stimulus to twitch a muscle and keep him from turning into a literal couch potato, Matt had been at the nerve-racking occupation of spoofing computer systems into disgorging data.

From the initial contact until he safely got away, he'd had to dodge various security programs and a couple of live systems managers. Matt felt limper than a cheap wash-rag after somebody had wrung it out and hung it up to dry. He literally wondered if he had the strength to get up, go to the bathroom, and throw some cold water on his face.

Worst of all, his whole effort had been for nothing. Matt's first move had been to consult the city directory, checking off every address which might overlook the corner he wanted. Then he had to search and see if any of those addresses had security cameras. Then came the job of hacking into the appropriate building systems and getting a look at the data for the date in question.

Bill Merrill KØEMJ
703 Hodge Ave.
Ames, Ia 50010.

AMES HAM MEETING

DOT BASEMENT

APRIL 6
THURSDAY
7:30 PM

PROGRAM

QSL SHOW&TELL
AND
NWA SEVERE WEATHER
CONFERENCE REPORT,

Bring your favorite QSL cards
Also a weather report from Jerry
Questions?
WØNFL sec. 515-232-0333

The result? Not one of the cameras actually recorded the corner of G Street and Wilson Avenue. A couple of yards off here, half a block off there. But if there was an angle that might show a waiting James Winters on that corner, he hadn't found it. Kind of weird, that. He'd have bet that it wasn't possible to find an unrecorded inch in that neighborhood.

Matt tried to get up and groaned.

This is what I get for breaking the law, he thought.

School would be coming all too soon. He'd probably walk the halls of Bradford Academy like some sort of zombie, one of the living dead. . . .

Dead . . . Matt closed his eyes again. It wasn't worth wasting the time to get up and go to bed. He could just lie here, doze for an hour or so . . .

At that moment his wallet decided to attack him from his back pocket.

Matt blinked, trying to push his tired mind to make sense of what was going on. Oh—the vibration was his wallet-phone. . . .

He dug the wallet out, switched to the foilpack keypad, and switched it to phone format.

"Hello?" His voice was more like a groan.

"Matt?" Even considering the wallet-phone's inherent shortcomings, the voice on this connection was incredibly tinny. It took Matt a moment to figure out who was calling.

Finally, "Squirt?" Matt squinted over for a look at his clock and flinched in horror. "Do you know what time it is? What are you doing up?"

"I—um—I was hacking," Mark Gridley confessed.

Well, I know how that feels, Matt thought.

Mark rushed on. "Sorry. I know this must sound kind of scraggy. I'm still on the Net. Figured this would be quieter than disconnecting and calling from a phone."

Matt could understand that. The vidphones didn't exactly ring selectively. And a parent awakened before daybreak was not a happy parent. His own folks wouldn't be pleased to discover that he'd spent the entire night out on the Net. The Squirt would probably get it worse than Matt would.

He was four years younger . . . and his father was the head of Net Force.

Mark was still babbling. "I knew that calling your house would probably wake everybody up. So I tried your wallet-phone, one of those hope-and-a-prayer things. I'm kind of surprised I got you."

In a reasonable universe I'd have been asleep in my pajamas, and the phone would have been gently vibrating on the top of my dresser, Matt thought.

Aloud, he said, "But you did get me. What was so important that you'd take a shot at waking me up before sunrise?"

"I couldn't copy the files I hacked into, and I want to share this while the memory is still fresh. It's about Captain Winters. I got the feeling that the I.A. report was holding stuff back. So I used some of Dad's codes and went into the Net Force computers . . . hello?"

Matt finally remembered to breathe out all the air he'd just sucked in. "You did *what?*" he asked in a strangled voice. *And here I was sweating over a bit of stupid, low-level hacking,* he thought.

"The stuff I got—it's not the I.A. report, but records from before—the time of the first bombing." Mark sucked in a breath of his own. "The time when the captain's wife was killed."

The more Mark talked, the wider Matt's eyes became. He stirred himself around, cued up his own computer, and began recording the story the Squirt was telling. He had a lot to learn from the kid. . . .

Megan was frankly annoyed to be attending another meeting of the D.C. crew. Not only was she wasting time watching everybody discuss what they should do, but they were wasting time she could have spent sharing information with Leif Anderson. They'd sealed their alliance last night by agreeing to a Net date this evening to go over *all* the information they'd dug up.

"I'm sorry to drag everybody in again," Matt greeted them.

"You sound like Agent Dork," Megan grumbled.

"The Sq—that is, Mark—came up with something last night," Matt went on. "I'll turn the floor over to him."

"If we had a floor," Andy Moore joked from where he floated in the void.

Mark Gridley was usually talkative, even cocky. But this evening he was strangely subdued. "I thought there were pieces of the Internal Affairs report that we weren't seeing, so I went in—"

"Where?" David asked.

"Where do you think?" Megan shot back.

David shut up, but there was a worried look on his face.

"There was nothing useful in the report, but there were other records that they were using to collate their findings with—stuff dating back to when Mrs. Winters was killed in the bomb blast." Mark took a deep breath. "Sealed court transcripts, internal memos, and the results of a Net Force disciplinary hearing."

"Who got disciplined?" Megan asked. She felt a sudden chill. "The captain didn't do something crazy back then, did he?"

"Captain Winters and his partner, 'Iron' Mike Steele, were investigating a mob-owned company that supposedly offered computer assistance to small businesses. What it actually did was drain them dry. If the owners realized this and tried to break the contract . . . well, this was Alcista's baby. They wound up with broken legs. Or worse." Mark looked sick. "It seems Alcista liked to get out in the field and show his leg-breakers how it was done. Winters and Steele were gathering evidence to show that besides running a criminal organization, Alcista had personally put several victims in the hospital.

"Somehow, Alcista found out and decided to stop the investigation by taking out both Net Force operatives. Bombs were placed in both Winters's and Steele's cars."

He shook his head. "Apparently, Mrs. Winters had an early doctor's appointment, and her car wouldn't start. She got behind the wheel of the captain's car, and . . . we know what happened then. There was time to warn Steele, so he never got in his car that day. Lucky thing, considering the bomb Net Force found. The problem was, no matter how hard they pressed, Net Force couldn't manage to link the bombing plot to Stefano Alcista."

"We know all that," Megan said impatiently. "That's why Alcista only took the rap for fraud and extortion."

But Mark was shaking his head. "That wasn't the story the court papers showed. Alcista was going to be arraigned on murder charges."

"How?" P. J. Farris demanded.

"When Net Force couldn't pin the bombings on Alcista, Iron Mike came up with evidence that showed certain records had been deleted from Alcista's computer, but not completely destroyed. When Net Force techs brought them back, they definitely incriminated Alcista."

Megan frowned. "Then how——"

"It wasn't real," Mark Gridley said. "Steele got the nickname 'Iron Mike' not because he was so strong, but because people joked he was part machine. He was a specialist agent who could just about make computers sit up and bark on command."

He shook his head. "I was impressed at how he managed to plant the evidence. A seemingly innocent phone call inserted a very nasty program that called several incriminating numbers, then erased the records. Get it?"

Megan nodded. "But the traces would be left if anybody looked for them. And it would seem as if Alcista had tried to erase the evidence that would prove him guilty."

"Federal prosecutors were getting ready to try and put Alcista away for life. . . ." Mark hesitated. "Until Captain Winters found out that the evidence was false. He took the story straight to my father."

The nightscape they were floating in was quiet as the Net Force Explorers took that in.

"But—but——" Daniel Sanchez was so upset, his protest came out as a sputter. "Alcista *was* guilty. By blowing the whistle on the falsified evidence, Winters was letting his wife's killer walk."

Mark nodded. "That's exactly what happened. Not only

did the murder case crash and burn, it gave Alcista's lawyers the leverage to set up a pretty lenient deal for the charges that could stick."

"Which explains the closed court records," Leif said quietly. "No one would want the reason for the change in sentencing getting into the public record."

"So, instead of life, a killer gets a couple of years in a country-club prison," Megan said bitterly. "Talk about a slap on the wrist—"

"What happened to Steele?" Andy wanted to know.

"That was the disciplinary hearing," Mark said. "Pretty open-and-shut. Steele twisted the prime purpose of his job— the very reason Net Force was created. He was cashiered but disappeared before charges could be brought against him. Apparently, he was a boat nut. He took his cabin cruiser and headed south."

The Squirt shrugged. "About a month later the boat blew up in the Caribbean, with Steele aboard. There were some internal Net Force memos about whether it was accidental or deliberate." He shook his head. "Apparently, he'd told a lot of people that he preferred a Viking funeral, sailing into the sunset aboard a burning boat."

"Sounds like he got his wish," Andy said. "Even if he had to arrange it himself."

"Forget about all that stuff," Matt said excitedly. "Don't you see? This whole earlier episode proves that Captain Winters is innocent! He had a chance to screw over Alcista and not even get his hands dirty. Why would he plant a bomb after the guy got out of jail?"

"Take it from Steadman's point of view," Leif said harshly. "Winters does this tremendously noble thing, and his worst enemy gets sentenced as if he'd spat in the street instead of killing somebody. A couple of years go by, with Winters stewing over the unfairness of it all. Then Alcista gets out—and Winters sets out to get justice, no matter how belatedly."

Megan fought a chill as she stared at her supposed ally.

Leif shrugged. "Twist hard enough, and you can make any set of facts fit the pattern you've already decided on.

We see the captain's actions as proving his innocence. Steadman saw it as showing his guilt."

"Won't a jury get to decide all that?" Matt insisted. "The stuff Mark found shows Winters in an entirely different light from the picture the media is pounding into everyone's heads."

"Do you honestly want things to go that far? I don't. So what do you want to do with what we know?" Leif snapped. "Spread it around to every competitor HoloNews has? It would just be dismissed as wild rumor. We don't have any documentation we can show anybody."

Miserably Mark nodded. "I wasn't able to download anything without setting off alarms from here to Canada. Just getting in was hard enough."

Leif went on a little more quietly. "Besides, this isn't news to the one person who really counts. Captain Winters lived through it all. His lawyer could subpoena all the records Mark found, and maybe even petition the court to unseal the records on Alcista's sentencing deal."

He hesitated for a second. "If he wanted to."

"If?" Megan echoed. "*IF?* Don't you mean *when*? What are you talking about, Anderson? This is the captain's 'get out of jail free' ticket."

She stared uncomprehending at Matt's suddenly stricken expression. Out of all the kids in the room, Matt was probably the most like James Winters. So why wasn't he happy? What was wrong with this information that would exonerate the captain?

"If he uses it," Matt said in a hollow voice. "Here's a guy who basically let his wife's killer go rather than ruin Net Force's reputation for integrity. Do you think he's going to smear the agency now just to get *himself* off the hook?"

After the Squirt's bombshell of an announcement—and the
realization that it still didn't help their case—most of the
Net Force Explorers began synching out. Some stayed to
discuss the news a little, but it was clear their hearts weren't
in it.

Leif Anderson wasn't one of those. Something that had
been said during this get-together was teasing his brain. He
felt as though he were on the edge of an idea . . . just what
kind of idea, however, he couldn't say.

A thought sent him floating through Matt Hunter's starry
sky to where Megan O'Malley hung like a very pretty balloon.

"Well, this went much shorter than I expected," he said
quietly.

She nodded, her expression not a very happy one. Then
her eyes went sharp. "You've got that 'I'm hatching something' look," she told him.

"I'm not sure what it is," he admitted. "But I could use
your help finding out. You still want to meet?"

She nodded.

"Chez vous or *chez moi?"*

"Your place, I think," she replied.

Then it was Leif's turn to nod. Megan's workspace was impressive, a virtual amphitheater on one of the moons of Jupiter.

But its vastness wasn't the greatest place to share confidences.

Leif stretched out a hand, and Megan took it. In the blink of an eye they were in the living room of the Icelandic stave house he'd carved out of cyberspace. Leif dropped onto the sofa, surprisingly comfortable in spite of its angular, modernistic look. Megan joined him.

"Oh!" she said, glancing out the big window. "You run a night and day cycle in here." She turned from the view to him. "But it's not a full moon—is it?"

He shrugged. "I like a full moon."

"Good for romance," she said cynically.

"Maybe later. We were going to share information, remember?"

Megan gave him a half-smile. "I'll show you mine if you'll show me yours."

He pushed back a wave of annoyance. Megan was acting as if this were some kind of date, playing boy-girl games. Or maybe it was just that he realized he didn't have much to bargain with.

"You've already got most of what I dug up," he admitted. "Except for the source."

Megan looked skeptical. "Who is she, and why should I be interested?"

"Her name is Bodie—short for Boadicea—Fuhrman," Leif said in a resigned tone of voice. "She used to be an intern at HoloNews, working for Tori Rush. I happened to meet her the evening after she quit."

"And the morning after that, as I recall, you looked like you'd been run over by a truck," Megan said. "What is she, a female wrestler?"

Leif shook his head. "Just somebody who was determined to party hearty." He thought for a moment. "Everybody got so interested in what Tori Rush was doing—hiring detectives to dig up her stories—that they ignored *why* she was doing it."

"It's an old story," Megan said. "She wants a promotion."

"She wants her own show," Leif corrected. "Even has the name picked out—*The Rush Hour*."

Megan wrinkled her nose. "Cute, but a bit much," she said. "I guess Ms. Rush isn't in the running for the World's Smallest Ego award."

"Most people in show business aren't," Leif agreed. "And these days that includes network news as well. At least the on-air personalities."

"And your new friend Bodie—was she a budding personality as well?"

"More of a frustrated idealist," Leif suggested. "She's hoping for a job on *The Fifth Estate* when she gets out of school."

"So, you were already discussing her hopes and dreams," Megan said.

Leif could feel his face growing warm. Megan was *not* making this easy. "I thought you might like to tackle Ms. Fuhrman this time around."

"Tired of her already?"

"I thought she might react differently to you than to me," Leif said.

"No doubt," Megan replied dryly.

"You can use the same approach as you did with Wellman at *The Fifth Estate*," Leif pushed grimly onward. "The loyal Net Force Explorer trying to help the captain."

"And why did I pick the bodacious Bodie?"

"You're tracking down a list of people who left HoloNews," Leif suggested. "Specifically, people connected with *Once Around the Clock*."

"That might work," Megan admitted. "It's certainly worth a try." She gave Leif a look. "And that's all you were holding out?"

"A little later in the evening Bodie mentioned Tori Rush's contact at I-on Investigations. Someone named Kovacs."

Suddenly Megan was leaning forward on the couch, her

eyes excited. "Marcus Kovacs? He's the big cheese in the company—supposedly a financial guy rather than an investigator." She frowned. "So why is Tori Rush talking with him instead of the guy digging up the dirt?"

"Customer relations," Leif suggested. "Maybe he wants to make sure his famous client is happy. Or maybe he wants to keep an eye on someone who could land him in a nasty lawsuit."

"I don't think he'd inspire confidence," Megan said critically. "He doesn't even look like a detective."

"And how many detectives have you seen—outside of holo-mysteries?" Leif wanted to know. Then he leaned toward Megan, his glance sharpening. "Wait a minute! You've actually seen this Kovacs guy?"

Megan nodded. "When I was talking to Wellman, he was going over flatcopies of images to use in his story about Tori and I-on." She grinned. "I just happened to capture them onto my system."

For a second she just sat there on the couch, silently communing with her implant circuitry. When she turned to Leif again, she had a sheaf of papers in her hands.

"Here's the elusive Mr. Kovacs, in three pictures—two and a half," she amended, shuffling through the images, "unless you count the palm of his hand. Apparently, he's very camera-shy."

Leif took the pages and stared at the pictures. "Looks prosperous," he muttered, taking in the cut of the man's expensive suit jacket. An eagle-beak of a nose dominated his face, looking like an aiming device for deep brown eyes that almost looked black. As for the rest of the face . . . "I guess we should also mention hairy," he said.

"*Very* hairy," Megan agreed, tapping a finger on the graying jet-black mane. "When was the last time business-people wore their hair this long?"

"There was that whole revival of the ponytail thing when we were kids." Leif frowned, moving on to the next picture. "But that was for supposedly creative types—fashion designers, heads of Hollywood studios, public-relations geniuses."

"Lawyers, too, I thought," Megan put in.

"In holos, maybe," Leif said in disgusted tones. "I remember my father saying he'd never do business with what he called 'the ponytail boys.' He told me, 'Never trust anyone who's a slave to fashion—it means they can't think for themselves.' "

"Well then, maybe Mr. Kovacs is an original." Megan grinned. "Nobody is going around with a big mane of hair right now—unless it's a European thing."

"Not that I know of." Leif looked at the second image, where Kovacs had absently brushed back his hair. Then came the third, with the palm of Kovacs's hand filling most of the image space.

What is he hiding? Leif wondered.

Then the idea that had been tickling around the back of his brain began to come into focus. Take the stuff he'd been hearing about I-on Investigations. Mix it with what the Squirt had to say earlier this evening . . .

"Computer," he suddenly ordered, "Net search, public databases, concentrating on news sources. Images, Michael Steele, former Net Force specialist agent. Time frame—" He turned to Megan. "When was the captain's wife killed?"

"July 21, 2021," Megan said, baffled.

"Time frame, third and fourth week of July, 2021," Leif finished. "Execute."

"Working," a silvery female voice replied.

Megan rolled her eyes. "Even your computer has to be sexy."

"It's a proven fact," Leif said stiffly, "that men hear female voices more clearly."

"Unless they're saying something the men don't want to hear," Megan shot back.

Long minutes ticked by in silence. Leif had expected a bit of a wait—his search engine would probably have to access dead storage to dig up a four-year-old news story. But their prickly exchange made the down time seem interminable.

"All right," Megan finally said, "I'll bite. What are you doing?"

"It's a long shot," Leif had to admit. "We've got the head of a detective agency who creates evidence for a living. Four years ago we had a Net Force operative who got bounced from the agency for false evidence. Do you see a connection?"

"A very hazy one," Megan replied. "After all, one of those people is dead."

"Reported dead," Leif corrected her. "Suspected of having a Viking funeral far out at sea. How much would be left to identify after that?" He frowned. "A lot of Marcus Kovacs's past can't be checked, either. So I thought it would be interesting to see what both of our mystery men looked like, side by side."

"You did, did you?"

Before she could tell him what she thought of that idea, the computer's silvery voice chimed in. "Search completed. Eighteen matches."

"Have her say, 'Oh, baby,'" Megan suggested. "Just once."

Leif studiously ignored her, looking at the first of Megan's captured portraits of Marcus Kovacs. "Computer, are any of the matched images three-quarter views of the face?"

"Three," the computer responded.

"Display each. Format, nine inches by twelve inches," Leif said.

Three portraits popped into existence in front of them, all of them apparently shot on the fly. Each image showed the same grim-looking man, his hair cut so short it looked like a sandy fuzz on his skull. In contrast, Mike Steele's eyebrows were long and tangled, a solid line of darker hair stretching over his broken nose.

Megan made a raucous sound, somewhere between a buzz and a hoot. "AAAaaaarrrrkkkkk! You lose, monkey-boy. If you were ever hoping for a match with Marcus Kovacs, you definitely didn't get one!"

13

Megan cut the phone connection and scowled at her computer. Maybe she shouldn't have mocked Leif Anderson and his idea quite so heartlessly. She hadn't had a bit of luck in the two days since.

Leif had only shrugged at her laughter and downloaded a facsimile of the scrap of paper Bodie Fuhrman had given him—her name and number, a New York City phone code.

Megan glared at the printed flatcopy printout lying in front of her. The name and numbers were half printed, half cursive, in a round, bold, extremely feminine handwriting. It could be worse. At least Bodie didn't use a little heart to dot the *i* in her name.

The number turned out to be a phone in a Columbia dorm. The past few days hadn't exactly been a game of phone tag. It had been more like phone hide-and-seek. Megan would call and leave a message with one of Bodie's roommates. But Bodie herself would never call back.

What was the problem with these people? Megan wondered. Did they forget to pass the messages along? Megan had a couple of older brothers who had the same problem. Or was there a black hole in Bodie's computer memory

that ate any trace of call-back records? Maybe the roommates just left a paper note somebody's dog scarfed up.

Or could it be that Bodie Fuhrman was simply trying to
duck her?

Whatever the reason, Megan's patience was wearing
pretty thin by the time she finally caught up with the seemingly shy college girl.

Megan watched the image of a short, round-faced red-
head in a tight purple sweater giving her a blank look. "Oh,
yeah," Bodie finally said. "You're the kid who's been calling from Washington."

Kid? Megan thought, bristling at the older girl's conde-
scending attitude. *I'm the same age as Leif. And you certainly didn't seem to think he was a "kid."*

Of course, she couldn't say that, not without calling attention to the Anderson connection. Instead, Megan introduced herself as a Net Force Explorer trying to help Captain
Winters.

"You mean the guy who killed the gangster? I can't
imagine that anyone named Steve the Bull didn't get what
was coming to him," Bodie said. "But this country has a
little thing called due process. You've got to be able to
prove the guy guilty in court before you start punishing
him. Besides, do-it-yourself executions can be kind of
rough on innocent bystanders."

"My friends and I don't think the captain killed anybody," Megan began.

"Oh, please—he's innocent?" Bodie scoffed. "You
sound like the neighbors in any big ax-murder case. 'He
was such a nice, quiet man,' " she said in a quavering fal-
setto. " 'Always kept the lawn neatly mowed.' "

Bodie sneered. "Right. Until he mowed down half his
family—or, in this case—"

"We think your former boss framed him," Megan interrupted.

Well, at least Bodie wasn't laughing at her anymore. The
girl in the holographic display suddenly looked wary.
"What do you mean?"

"Tori Rush has been trying to turn herself into a star

attraction, churning out scandal stories for the past few months. The question is, did she order her pit-bull detectives to do a job on someone from Net Force? Or did they come to her, offering Captain Winters's head on a silver platter? And just how far did I-on Investigations go to set up the story in the first place?"

Bodie Fuhrman's green eyes flared, but her voice was almost prim as she answered. "It would certainly be inappropriate for me to comment on that. I have no knowledge one way or the other."

Megan wanted to reach through the holo connection and shake the other girl. A man's life and freedom were on the line here. And Bodie was treating the whole situation as if she were on some stupid interview show.

Interview . . . Suddenly Megan understood it all. Why Bodie was so hard to get hold of. Why she'd tried to blow Megan off, feeding her heaping helpings of hot and cold attitude. Why she was playing word games instead of answering Megan's questions now.

Bodie had obviously had a chat with Professor Arthur Wellman. The college girl was trying to maintain a low profile until her big Tori Rush story broke in *The Fifth Estate*.

I'll give her a low profile, a furious Megan thought. *In fact, I'll flatten that fat face for her.*

She took off the verbal gloves, mentioned Wellman's name, pressed hard—and got a raised voice, a rather uninspired collection of curse words, and a quick cutoff for her trouble.

What a bitch! Megan thought. *How could Leif stand her?*

She was still scowling at her system when the chimes rang, indicating an incoming message. She picked up and got a glimpse of red hair as the image swam into resolution. For an instant she thought it was Bodie Fuhrman calling back for round two.

Instead, it was Leif Anderson.

"I finally got to talk with your girlfriend," Megan announced ominously. "All I can say is, I hope you've been spending your time more constructively than I have."

Leif shrugged. "Can't exactly say that. I'm still playing with those pictures you gave me."

Megan rolled her eyes. "Trying to prove that a pair of guys who could win the Tag-Team Least Lookalike Award are in fact the same person? You're wasting—"

"Am I?" he asked. "Synch in and come to my place. You have to take a look at this."

Muttering, Megan sank into her computer-link couch and let her implanted circuits take over. An instant later she opened her eyes in the living room of Leif's virtual dream house.

Instead of lounging on one of the pieces of furniture, as he usually did, Leif was on his feet and facing her. Everything about him—his expression, his posture—showed his eagerness over what he was about to show her.

Megan hoped he wasn't about to make a fool of himself—or of her.

Leif gave a command to his computer, and two headings appeared on either side of him in glowing light: "Marcus Kovacs" and "Michael Steele." Then lists appeared under each name.

MARCUS KOVACS	MICHAEL STEELE
Hair: black/long	Hair: sandy/short
Eyebrows: thin	Eyebrows: heavy
Nose: aquiline	Nose: broken
Eyes: brown	Eyes: blue
Age: Mid-forties	Age: Mid-forties
Build: brawny	Build: brawny
Suit size: 44	Suit size: 44
Left-handed	Left-handed
Blood type: AB−	Blood type: AB−

Megan dismissed the list with a glance. "Very nice," she said. "Are you going to do one for the two of us now? We've got about as much in common."

"I wouldn't say that," Leif said. "Take a closer look. The first four features on the list—the externals—couldn't be more different. But they're also easily handled by artificial means. Hair dye, eyebrow clipping, plastic surgery, and contact lenses—"

"Eyebrow clipping?" Megan scoffed.

"Oh, right, as if girls never reshape their own eyebrows," Leif replied. "I know of at least one male Hollywood star who had to have his eyebrows plucked, or they made him look like the Wolf Man." He pointed to the lower part of the list. "The things down here—fundamentals—are things you can't change so easily. And every characteristic matches perfectly."

Megan stared at Leif. He'd certainly gone off the deep end this time. "How many people are a size forty-four in this country? In the world? And even if AB negative is a comparatively rare blood type, when you look at the blood type as a proportion of the current U.S. population, millions of people have it. That's not a small number."

"I'm aware of that," Leif said. "That list just represents the groundwork."

She looked at him. "For what?"

"With the help of your pictures, the ones I searched out—and some holo imagery I managed to dig up—I created these."

The lists on either side disappeared. Now Leif was flanked by two men—Marcus Kovacs and Michael Steele.

"What—" Megan began.

"Three-D sims," Leif interrupted with some satisfaction. "Life-size, so we can really start looking for similarities. By the way, did you know that Kovacs and Steele are the same height and wear the same size shoe?"

"Tell me more, Sherlock," Megan said in a resigned kind of voice. "At least they're wearing clothes, so I guess you didn't find any identifying moles on somebody's butt."

"They tell me you can find lots of *revealing* pictures on the Net." Leif grinned. "But certainly not of either of these guys."

"Thank heaven," Megan muttered.

Leif gave another order, and his new friends swung around to present their profiles. "It's hard to tell because of that full beard that Kovacs wears, but I think both men have the same basic shape face and chin."

"At least, you'd like to think so." Megan tried to choose what she was about to say carefully. It wasn't easy: words like *silly, stupid,* and *crackpot* came all too easily to her sometimes too-blunt tongue. "Leif, you want to find someone behind all the *merde* Captain Winters is going through. I might even say you're desperate. So am I. If you can't convince me, when I *want* to clear the captain, how are you going to convince Matt, or David, or . . . say . . . Captain Steadman?"

"Let me show you one other thing," Leif begged. "Remember how bent out of shape Kovacs got in the last picture you showed me? The one where he stuck his hand over the camera lens?"

Megan felt a surge of hope. "Fingerprints?"

Leif shook his head. "Nothing but the lines on the palm—although they *do* match. But remember what Kovacs was doing in the picture before that?"

"Brushing his hair back—"

"So you could see his ear." Leif murmured another command. Both sims wheeled around to face his left. "This is the side the camera-person caught." He reached over to the make-believe Kovacs and pulled back the thick, graying mane to reveal the simulacrum's left ear. Another command, and the sim of Mike Steele disappeared.

No, wait, Megan realized, *it wasn't gone.* It had been superimposed over the Kovacs clone. The end result was sort of surprising. The lines of the men's foreheads matched, except for the differing eyebrows. The noses were different, but the lips were the same, as far as she could tell beneath that beard.

"What am I supposed to be looking for?" she asked.

"The ears," Leif said excitedly. "They're supposed to be the most difficult part of the body to disguise."

Megan peered hard at the superimposed holograms. To her surprise, the two men's ears matched perfectly.

"It may not be a set of matching moles on their butts,

but I think it's pretty convincing." Leif gave her a smug smile.

Megan had to admit, Leif had come up with a good presentation with the two images occupying the same space. Where their shapes disagreed, the image was misty and insubstantial. For instance, Kovacs's beard was a gossamer gray outgrowth surrounding the equally ghostly chin of Michael Steele.

The forehead and lips—and the placement of the eyes, she now noticed—looked as concrete as if a real person stood before her.

Megan turned her attention back to those ears. They were large enough but didn't stick out as much as, say, Agent Len Dorpff's.

The tops of Kovacs's and Steele's ears were slightly pointed, giving just the hint of elf ears. The skin-covered cartilage, with its bumps, twists, and ridges, even the fleshy earlobe below, looked exactly solid. No trace of ghosting or double image betrayed any differences, standing up even to her most searching gaze.

Megan felt a little weird, peering so intently into somebody's ear, even if it was a sim. Well, it wasn't as if the Kovacs-Steele sim was going to turn around and yell "Boo!"

At least, it better not, she told herself, *if Leif values his health.*

"Amazing," she finally said, turning to Leif. "They even seem to have the same amount of ear wax."

More seriously, she went on. "I have no idea what the chances are of identical ears turning up on people. But I suspect it narrows the field a lot more than shoe size or blood type. And you say it's almost impossible to disguise an ear? Where did you learn that?"

Leif's smug expression slipped a little. "I think it was an old flatfilm movie—or was it a TV show?"

Megan sighed. "Let's see if you can back that up with something a little more scientific. Then we'll take your wax museum to Matt Hunter for a look-see."

14

Leif looked back and forth between the two friends sitting in his virtual living room.

Megan looked as though she were having second thoughts about discussing the mysterious similarities between Marcus Kovacs and "Iron Mike" Steele.

And Matt Hunter acted more as though Leif were burglarizing the house instead of paying a friendly visit over the Net.

Matt must have caught Leif's surprised look. "My parents think I'm studying," he said. "With all the stuff I've been doing to help the captain—well, I really got nailed on a couple of tests."

Leif and Megan nodded somberly. Their grades, too, had suffered as a result of all-nighter Net sessions, long-distance calls, and meetings over how to help Captain Winters.

"I know what you mean," Megan said. "My folks are just about ready to lower the boom on me, too. Unless something looks as if it's going to pan out, and really quickly, this will be my last full-scale shot at helping the captain for a while. I've got to get my grades up, or I'll be grounded so long I'll be collecting retirement before I can venture out again."

Matt nodded unhappily. "Me, too. So, you two, what have you got?"

"Tell him, Leif," Megan said.

Leif glanced at her. Yes, she was definitely getting cold feet. He'd only half-convinced her last night, and now her confidence was leaking like a soda bottle hit with a load of buckshot. Even though he'd shown her the passage in the FBI manual about ear shape being a prime identifier, and admissible in court. The usefulness of ear shape in identifying a disguised suspect was why people in mug shots and on wanted posters had their hair pulled back in the profile shot. The authorities wanted that information on record. Meg had heard, she had read, but she was obviously having a hard time believing.

Calling up his lists of similarities, Leif began his dog-and-pony show.

Megan was also right. Matt was even harder to convince than she was.

"Do I get what you're trying to say here?" Matt said in disbelief. "You want me to believe that these two people are the same guy? Or, rather, that Marcus Kovacs is 'Iron Mike' Steele?"

"Let me just point out a couple of things," Leif replied to his skeptical friend. "According to his paper trail, Marcus Kovacs is supposed to be a financial guy—what my father calls a bean-counter. Yet he's going great guns as the head of a detective agency. That would sound like more of a job for Mike Steele, late of Net Force, trained in the special facilities at the FBI's Quantico Academy."

" 'Late' is right," Matt shot back. "Mike Steele is dead, remember? He had a Viking funeral."

"Correction. Mike Steele was declared dead on an island down in the Caribbean, because people saw his boat burn up and sink. Nobody actually saw *him* die. I checked the story out with some insurance-company people. They mentioned that that part of the world is a favorite place for people to go to pretend they've kicked the bucket so they can collect on their life insurance policies. The water's warm enough, and plenty of other islands are close enough for the 'corpse' to make a nice, easy swim to another waiting boat. If Iron Mike wanted to bail, he chose the perfect place to do it."

"And what about Marcus Kovacs? You gonna tell me that his whole life is made up, a paper trail? He's got a valid birth certificate. Didn't anybody see him get born?"

"You'd have a hard time finding witnesses," Leif said. "The village where Kovacs was supposedly born got smeared by both sides during the Sava River campaign. There's no town hall left—it was flattened; no church . . . no records at all, really. Paper hardcopies of whatever documents the refugees had were submitted to the central government, when a new database was set up. The authorities had to take a lot of things on trust."

"So Kovacs is a figment of a computer's imagination?"

Leif shook his head. "He could have been a real person, born in that ghost town and getting a university degree. He'd have been just the right age to fight in the war that created the Free State. But a lot of people died in that war in thousands of little guerrilla actions—and, again, neither side has great records."

He looked at Matt. "The fact is, neither side keeps such great records even now. The Carpathian Alliance is under serious trade embargo, so they can't get decent computers. And the Free State is too poor to afford the newest machines—or the security software to protect them."

Leif pounced on Matt's expression of surprise. "Given a reasonable knowledge of the language, a good hacker could easily penetrate government computers over there and insert a whole life story. Or rather, a life story in fragments, just like almost everyone else's."

Matt still wasn't coming over. Leif could see it in his face.

"Remember," Leif said, "Steele got the nickname 'Iron Mike' because people kidded that he was part computer. He was a specialist agent whose job was to penetrate systems and uncover information for the good guys. It would be easy for him to plant whatever he needed in the old crap they're using in the Balkans."

He stabbed a finger at his friend. "And it would explain how this bean counter became so good at computer investigation. More important, what caused Mike Steele's downfall in Net Force?"

"Falsifying evidence," Matt admitted.

"And what is I-on Investigations making its big profits on?"

"Fake evidence," Megan said.

"I'll give you something else. Marcus Kovacs is known as Marc to his friends and associates."

"So?" Matt said.

"Marc . . . Mike. They sound awfully alike, don't they? It makes life easier for someone who adopts an alias. That's why the majority of Witness Protection program people pick sound-alike names or use the same initials."

"Your analogy breaks down, then," Matt said. "Mike Steele—Marc Kovacs? What sort of connection is that?"

Leif shrugged. "Not much of one in English. But Kovacs is a Hungarian name. In that language it means 'smith.' "

"Oh, great," Megan said. "America's most popular alias on motel records."

"You still don't get it," Leif said. "Smith—as in 'blacksmith'—somebody who works on iron . . . and steel."

His friends stared at him for a long moment, until Matt finally broke the silence. "Pretty clever, Leif. But you're hanging a lot of *what-if*s on this guy's—or maybe these guys'—ears."

"The basis for that leap is in the FBI manual," Leif began wearily. "And I'm just raising some possibilities. The world is full of professional investigators—some of whom may even be honest. It will be up to them to prove or disprove what I'm suggesting."

"Up to them?" Megan repeated.

"We're not the Junior Net Force, you know," Leif pointed out. "We don't have police powers. We just poke around and ask questions. And something tells me that it would be smarter—and maybe healthier—to let the pros take a shot at poking around Marcus Kovacs."

"You think what you have here will be enough to turn Steadman and Internal Affairs around?" Disbelief was plain in Matt's voice.

"No," Leif admitted. "But I think an honest private eye, directed by, say, Captain Winters's lawyer, might do some good. At the very least my theory offers a possible defense at a trial. Better than anything the captain has been able to come up with so far, which is mainly to say, 'I didn't do it!' "

He gave Matt a straight look. "Captain Winters is innocent. We know that. So we also know that Winters has been set up by someone who does very good work. You tried and couldn't shake any part of the I.A. case."

"I couldn't help the captain," Matt admitted.

"But using this information, a lawyer might be able to make a case for a frame-up job," Leif said. "Right down to a well-trained perpetrator with motive and opportunity. Alcista died as punishment for trying to blow up Steele. Winters could have been framed as punishment for letting the cat out of the bag when Steele phonied up evidence against Alcista."

"All this talk about lawyers is fine, but we don't even know who has the job of representing the captain," Megan objected.

"Stewart Laird," Leif promptly answered. "He's a partner in Mitchell, Liddy, and Laird, a firm of criminal lawyers—"

"You'd think they'd come up with a different way to refer to that," Megan interrupted. "It makes the lawyers sound like crooks."

Leif chuckled. "Point taken." Then he grew more serious. "It's a small outfit. They're not power brokers like some of the big Washington law firms. But these guys know their business, which is what Winters needs. I was afraid I'd find him represented by some ambulance chaser, or the guy who handled the mortgage on his house."

"How did you find out about this lawyer?" Megan wanted to know. "I haven't seen his name or the firm's mentioned on any newscasts or in any of the print media."

Leif gave a quick command to the computer. Instantly one end of the living room turned into a view of a large, crowded office, with a pretty brunette sitting behind a desk at the foreground. "Hi, I'm Tracey McGonigle?" she said, a classic California upward lilt at the end of the sentence making it sound like a question. "I'm working for FaxNews International? We're trying to get in touch with the lawyer representing James Winters?"

Megan turned on Leif with a dangerous expression. "That—that cardboard cutout looks like an older version of *me!* Although it doesn't sound like me—thank heaven."

"I didn't think any law firm would deal with a teenager," Leif said. "But with someone slightly older, working for an obscure news organization—"

"Do you have a sim program that makes all of us look older?" Megan demanded.

Matt, however, wasn't about to get distracted. "You launched this program to contact every law firm in the Greater Washington metropolitan area?"

"What a scam!" Megan shook her head in disbelief.

"A stratagem," Leif corrected her. "I started out in the Maryland suburbs and downtown D.C., figuring that those were the places Winters was most likely to go. Most of the firms either informed Ms. McGonigle that they weren't involved in the case, or turned her down flat. Mitchell, Liddy, and Laird's receptionist told young Tracey that Mr. Laird had no comment at this time."

"I see," Megan said. "I'm not going to ask if you have no shame. I already know the answer to that question. At least lawyers are safer to poke around than Kovacs or Steele."

"We need to present what we've found to Captain Winters's lawyer," Leif said. "I found out which partner we've got to call." He turned to Matt. "But I'd like you to do the talking."

"Why?" Matt asked suspiciously.

"Well, *I* can't, because they'd think my alias was Tracey McGonigle," grumped Megan. "It's hard to preserve a good reputation with a bunch of lawyers when they've got solid proof you're a scam artist."

Leif shook his head. *She's never going to let me live this one down,* he thought.

Aloud, he said to Matt, "Because you have a good reputation with Net Force . . . and with Captain Winters." He turned a mirthless grin toward Megan. "You heard Ms. O'Malley. If Winters heard this from me, he'd probably dismiss it without even listening. You, on the other hand, he might just listen to right through to the end. Admit it— it's an improvement over claiming innocence without a shred of an alibi."

"Huh," Matt said a little bitterly. "You want me to tell Captain Winters and his lawyer because everybody thinks I'm a goody-goody."

"I want you because you stand a good chance of being believed," Leif insisted. "If this Laird guy contacts Agent Dorpff, Dorpff'll give you a good recommendation. Dorpff doesn't know anything about me." He hesitated. "Or if he does, I'll bet it's not complimentary."

"So you want to scam this lawyer using my reputation," Matt began.

"This isn't a scam—this is Captain Winters's best hope. I want Laird to hear everything we've dug up," Leif said angrily. "I don't know what Winters has told him, but it's obvious to me from what we're seeing in the media that the law firm isn't undertaking a vigorous defense. We've got a blizzard of news items about the case, all from the prosecution's point of view. The folks at HoloNews do their poor best to *sound* fair. They refer to Winters as an 'alleged' murderer who's 'under investigation,' but the subtext in every report they file is 'he dunnit.' "

He was trying not to shout in frustration as he confronted his two friends. "The way things are going right now, unless this lawyer pulls off a miracle, Captain Winters will go to trial. He will probably be convicted. We know he's innocent. We've got to do something."

"You're right," Matt said. "You've got your patsy."

●　　●　　●

The next morning, during a break between classes, Matt phoned the number Leif had given him. "Mitchell, Liddy, and Laird," a female voice announced over his wallet-phone.

"My name is Matthew Hunter." Matt had to fight to keep his voice from rising at the end of the sentence like Leif's fictitious Tracey McGonigle. "I'm a Net Force Explorer, and I understand that Mr. Laird at your firm is representing the Net Force Explorer liaison officer, Captain James Winters. We've been trying to help the captain, and we've found out a couple of things that Mr. Laird might want to know."

The receptionist's voice was not encouraging. "I'm afraid Mr. Laird is very busy—"

"I don't expect Mr. Laird will talk to me right off the bat," Matt said. "But he might check on me with Net Force agent Len Dorpff and with his client, Captain Winters. I think either discussion would change Mr. Laird's mind." Matt gave the number for Captain Winters's old office. That's where Dorpff would be. He figured the lawyer should have Captain Winters's home number. "I'll call again later this afternoon. Perhaps Mr. Laird will speak to me then."

"Mr. Hunter!" At least Matt managed to surprise a human response out of the receptionist. "Wait!" Matt merely gave Agent Dorpff's number again, to make sure it was recorded properly.

Then he cut the connection.

By the time he got home after school, Matt was suffering from a bad case of sweating palms. For what had to be the fiftieth time on the trip home, he tapped the pocket containing the datascrip that Leif Anderson had prepared. Matt still wasn't sure if he had the gumption to pass along his friend's wild theory—

The autobus came to a stop on Matt's corner, and he got off. As he unlocked the door of his house, he heard the chime of an incoming call. Mom and Dad were both away at work. Matt dashed into the hall to the nearest holo receiver.

He made the connection, and the image of a face swam into focus on the system's display—a stranger's face. A lean-faced man with no-nonsense eyes looked silently at Matt for a long moment. "Matt Hunter?" the man finally said.

Matt nodded.

"I'm Stewart Laird. I understand you called my office this morning in regard to James Winters."

"I represent a group of Net Force Explorers—" Matt began.

Laird nodded. "So I understand from Agent Dorpff—and from my client. Captain Winters spoke very favorably of you." The lawyer frowned, then spoke again. "It was the first time he'd been forthcoming since he engaged my services."

When Laird cleared his throat and hesitated again, Matt began to realize that the lawyer was uncomfortable.

I wonder if he's got sweaty palms, Matt thought.

"I called you because I'll listen to whatever you have to say, but first I want to ask a favor," Laird finally said. "Mr. Winters—that's how he's been referring to himself of late—has all but barricaded himself inside his house, using a screening system to ignore most calls. I'd like you to go and see him."

"I don't know." Now it was Matt's turn to hesitate. "The last time I went out there . . ."

His voice trickled off.

Stewart Laird nodded. "I know what happened during your last visit. But I also know that when he spoke about you, James Winters actually became animated. I hadn't seen him act that way since the Net Force Internal Affairs report was issued."

The lawyer was doing his best to maintain a poker face, but Matt could see the concern in the man's eyes. "Some people think that all a good legal defense requires is an effective lawyer to argue the case. Your friend Mr. Winters should know better. An apathetic client can sabotage a case as badly, or worse, than an inept attorney."

Laird's eyes snapped. "I am *not* inept. In fact, I have a

reputation for being good at what I do. If you want to help James Winters's defense, you might pay him a visit. My office will bear the charge of round-trip car service."

The look Laird now sent Matt could almost be called pleading. "I've had clients who were innocent, and clients who were guilty. I think I can tell the difference. It . . . concerns me when I see an innocent man seem to lose all sense of hope."

15

Matt had barely finished the note telling his parents where he'd be when the gleaming car provided by the law firm rolled up outside his house. Almost before he had time to think about what he'd agreed to, he was in the Dodge sedan on his way to the Maryland suburb where James Winters lived.

The good news was that the driver was beating the rush-hour traffic. The bad news was every minute of this smooth trip brought Matt that much closer to his face-to-face meeting with the captain. Matt wasn't sure what he would find when he arrived. But it wasn't likely to be good. Stewart Laird had not struck him as a man who was easily shaken.

Obviously, the way James Winters was taking the developments in the murder case had his lawyer worried.

Not Captain Winters, but Mr. Winters, Matt thought. *That has to be a bad sign.*

The driver finally broke the tense silence. "You a witness or something?" he asked.

"What?" Wrestling with his thoughts, Matt had barely heard the question.

"I asked if you were a witness or something," the driver

repeated. "Usually, we wind up shuttling people who work late in the office, with the occasional personal delivery or family emergency. I know all of the partners' kids, so that lets you out on the last bit. You look like you're going to blow a valve back there, so I figured maybe you're some kind of surprise witness the firm is keeping under wraps for a big case."

For a crazy minute Matt felt the desire to go along with the guy. He could probably spin out some sort of story. After all, his folks were always watching courtroom holodramas. It would take his mind off . . .

But that brought his mind right back to the problem he would face when this ride was over.

"A friend of mine is in trouble," Matt finally said. "I've been asked to talk to him, to help put his mind at ease."

"Yeah, kids today, always getting into something weird. Myself, I blame the Net. Back when I was a kid, all we had was TV and the movies. You guys may laugh at the old stuff as 'flatfilm,' but that was *real* entertainment. We never had problems back then. . . ."

Right, Matt thought. *Back when Washington had the highest per capita murder rate of any city in the country.*

He let the driver talk on, thinking Matt was going to visit another teenager, until they finally arrived in Winters's neighborhood.

"Huh," said the driver. "Nice enough area. Isn't that always the way?"

He pulled up on the street. "I'll wait for you here until you're finished." The man gave him a conspiratorial wink. "No need to hurry. It's all on the law firm's tab."

Matt took a deep breath and walked up the drive. The last time he'd been here—barely two weeks ago—the place had been crawling with Net Force I.A. technicians. Now Winters's house looked deserted. The lawn was overgrown, obviously way past due for mowing, and the flower beds needed weeding.

I guess the captain isn't coming outside to take care of yardwork, Matt thought.

Mr. Winters, Matt corrected himself.

Well, he probably wouldn't want to mow, or paint, or even bring out the garbage, if that meant having people stare at him as if he were an animal in the zoo. Or, worse, if they were trying to thrust microphones into his face and ask him inane questions.

Winters had clearly disappointed the camera crews posted outside the house by not offering holo opportunities of any sort. At least the network vans were gone now, working the standard news cycle on some other story. An old saying popped into Matt's head. "The moving finger writes and, having writ, moves on."

Except in this case it was more like "The news ruins a life, and having ruined, moves on."

What was he going to find inside this house?

Matt reached the door and rang the bell. No answer. He should have realized it wouldn't be as easy as all that. How many reporters, camera crews, photographers, and just plain curious idiots had rung this bell since Winters's appearance on *Washington People?*

Actually, Matt was surprised to hear the faint sound of chimes inside. If he'd had to put up with this much nonsense, he'd have disconnected the doorbell.

Unless, of course, the chimes were announcing an incoming call. . . .

Matt waited a minute. No chimes. Then he hit the button and heard the faint sound. Okay, he wasn't just standing out here like an idiot.

No, he was. Winters wasn't answering his bell.

Matt tried a couple more short taps. Then he had it. He stretched out his thumb and just leaned on the bell. The faint sound of never-ending chimes seemed to travel up his arm.

The briefest movement at the window caught his attention. The drawn drapes had twitched. Someone was taking a look outside.

Matt let up on the bell, and a second later the door opened. There stood James Winters, staring at him.

Well, at least the captain's still shaving, Matt thought. He'd had this wild mental image of Winters turning into a stereotypical hermit, with long hair, a beard, and wild, red-rimmed eyes.

James Winters's face was thinner, the flesh seemingly stretched tighter over the bones of his skull. There were a few new lines at his eyes and on his brow. His expression was full of surprise as he took in his visitor.

"Matt!" Winters said. His voice had a strange, rusty sound to it.

Not surprising, Matt realized. If the man was staying in his house and not answering the door or the phone, who would he talk to, except himself?

And that might not be a good thing.

Winters seemed to remember his manners. "Come in!" he invited. "Sorry about the door. Last time I bothered to answer, there was some jackass with a camera and an autograph book. Called himself a murder buff. I was almost tempted to let him see how a murder worked—firsthand."

The captain's face set in bitter lines. "I mean, it couldn't do me any more damage than when this travesty goes to court."

They went into the living room. Matt was caught a little off-guard to see that the computer system had been removed. Then again, why should that be a surprise? It meant the room would be free of incoming calls and network news. Of course, it also meant no entertainment or research. If Winters was doing any preparation for his trial, he wasn't doing it here.

But there were traces of occupancy. Books lay on various pieces of furniture, several of the volumes resting facedown and open. Matt's mother hated to see that. "It breaks the bindings," she complained. "We're not going to have these things around forever, so let's not be in a hurry to destroy them."

Then Matt spotted something familiar on the sofa. It was a large, cylindrical scroll of paper—the statement of support Matt had delivered with the signatures of all the Net Force Explorers. He remembered how clumsy the bulky package had been to carry. Now it was undone, loose, and somewhat crumpled, as if it had been unrolled and read many, many times.

Matt could feel his face grow warm.

Winters came up behind him and followed his gaze. "You're looking at the relic?" he asked.

"Relic?" Matt echoed.

"A fossil, from the long-lost days when I could say something and people would believe me."

"We still believe you," Matt said. "All the Net Force Explorers believe you, Captain."

"Mister," Winters cut in. " 'Captain' is a Net Force title. Another relic." He shook his head. "All those years on the job, and it disappears in less than a week. People you risked your life for—and with—suddenly don't know you—"

"I've talked to the Squirt—Mark Gridley—his dad believes in you, too. He just can't speak out—"

"Oh, yes, political concerns. You see a lot of those in Washington. I'm sure I've got a personal message from him somewhere in the answering system."

It wasn't the words that chilled Matt's soul—although they were pretty upsetting. Even more upsetting was the bleak, lost look in Winters's eyes as he spoke.

This wasn't the James Winters Matt knew—sometimes stern, sometimes sharp-tongued, with a quick sense of humor and a tremendous concern for the young people entrusted to him.

This was a man who'd been dragged through the mud and then kicked a few times while he was down. He was wounded, and it showed.

Matt felt Winters's eyes resting on him. "So, this situation is most intriguing. My lawyer called earlier today. Counselor Laird was quite insistent on getting me to the phone. He wanted to ask me about one Matthew Hunter. Afternoon comes, and the same Matthew Hunter appears at my door. Coincidence? I think not."

Captain Winters responded to the look on Matt's face with a lopsided smile. "I can still add two and two and get some sort of answer, Matt. And you can tell Laird I'd better not see a bill with your cab fare on it. What can he stick it under? 'Restoring the client's spirits?' "

Winters carefully moved the scroll off the couch, put it on the coffee table, and sank down onto the cushions. "Sit. I really *am* glad to see you. However, since Laird was checking you out just hours ago, I must believe that he didn't search for you. Which means you came to him. Or to take it further, it means you're acting as a respectable front for whoever dug up the information that I'm being represented by Mitchell, Liddy, and Laird. So who's behind it, Matt? The crafty Mr. Anderson or the impetuous Ms. O'Malley?"

Matt had to hide a grin. Certainly, events hadn't robbed Captain Winters of his investigative talent.

"I'm afraid it's the worst-case scenario," he responded. "Both of them, aided and abetted along the way by most of the familiar faces in the D.C. group."

For just a second the old Captain Winters was present with the quick flash of a grin. "Figures," he said.

Matt chose his words carefully. "We've been trying to help you."

Matt went into some of what they had attempted: Leif's penetration of HoloNews, Megan's talks with *The Fifth Estate,* and Matt's own effort to back up Winters's alibi by hacking into the security camera files.

The captain's wry expression turned a bit more serious when he heard of this. "Agent Dorpff has a lot to learn about controlling his charges," Winters said. "Or am I just now learning about how much I've failed over the years?"

"Ummm, there's more," Matt pushed on. "Things we, uh, discovered about the earlier Alcista case that never made the news."

"Meaning those discoveries had to come from Net Force records," Winters rumbled. "Which would get a certain young hacker in severe trouble if his parents and Net Force ever found out."

Winters was more his old, stern self as he glared at Matt.

"Given the hacker, I think that discovery's unlikely, sir," Matt said.

"You've been taking quite an interest in my private business, it seems." Captain Winters looked at Matt searchingly. But then it seemed as though something inside him collapsed.

The captain's shoulders sank. "But you still didn't get the whole story," he said. "There are bits that even Net Force never got into the record. But I'll tell you everything, if you'd like. I guess sitting shut up in here has put me in a talkative mood."

Winters leaned back against the overstuffed back of the couch, but his tight muscles belied his casual pose. "Four years ago, my brilliant partner and I were hot on the trail of a piece of human garbage who offered computer services, and then used his access to steal people's businesses or whatever worthwhile assets they had. We were closing in on the guy, just shy of dropping the net on him. One rather gray April morning my wife's car wouldn't start, so she borrowed mine."

"To go to the doctor," Matt said.

Winters looked at him, his face as hard—and gray—as stone. "To be precise, she was going to our obstetrician. We were expecting . . . our son would have been born—"

He broke off, and Matt sat in horrified silence. Captain James Winters hadn't suffered one loss, but two—Mrs. Winters and their unborn child. Matt couldn't even begin to imagine what that had been like.

"Mike Steele was supposed to be the godfather. He'd already given us a baby present. Cynthia—my wife—had scolded him, saying it was bad luck. . . ."

Winters ran a hand over his face, but he at least looked calmer when he met Matt's eyes again. "I can understand why Mike did what he did. It wasn't just because Alcista had placed a bomb in his car. But when I learned the truth about the evidence he'd supposedly uncovered, I couldn't let the trial go on. I had to turn in my best friend. And let my wife's killer walk. Alcista's very expensive lawyers jumped in. By the time they were finished, Steve the Bull got a sentence that was more like a four-year vacation— three years and change—than a prison term. And I ended up with this huge hole where my life had been."

The captain's expression softened as he looked at his young listener. "Then came a bit of luck. Jay Gridley had me come in to his office for a talk. I told him I was burnt out as a field agent, and I didn't want to drive a desk in the administrative section. He said he had a special job that needed doing, and that he thought I was just the man for it. I became the liaison for the Net Force Explorers."

Matt cleared his throat. "We always suspected it was more than a job for you."

Winters nodded. "It was a lifeline during terrible times. You guys were so young, so enthusiastic, so . . . spirited."

"You mean out of control, don't you?"

"Maybe."

Matt seemed to see his mentor through completely new eyes. Now he understood why the captain was so tough when the Net Force Explorers bent the law in the cases where they'd become involved. Matt also understood why Winters took every Net Force Explorer so seriously when they came to him for advice. In a very real sense, he treated them like family. Maybe they were his family, the only family he had.

The captain gave Matt a surprisingly shy smile. "It's like that guy in the old book. I didn't have one child—I had thousands."

Then the captain's smile faded away. "But I've lost even that. I can almost laugh at how things turned out . . . almost. Just before the toilet flushed on me, Net Force asked me if I wanted to go back full-time on active duty. I turned the offer down because I was happy doing what I was doing. Now, even if by some miracle I beat the charges they're preparing against me, I'll be finished in Net Force. Which means I'm finished with the Net Force Explorers."

Slowly James Winters got control of his face and became the apathetic stranger who had answered the door. "I guess I feel betrayed." He sighed. "What goes around, comes around. I still remember the look in Iron Mike's eyes when he realized who had turned him in. Now I can understand it better."

His lips curved in a bleak smile. "You know, if anybody could have done this job on me, it would have been Iron Mike Steele. . . . Of course, he's not alive. But he's the only person it would make sense would be responsible."

Moving almost as though they had a will of their own, Matt's fingers went to the pocket that held Leif Anderson's datascrip.

"What—" Matt had to clear his throat to get the words out. "What if Mike Steele were still alive?"

"He died down in the Caribbean, on his boat." Winters shook his head. "Mike loved his boats. I used to kid him that that was why he stayed single—he couldn't afford a boat and a family, too. The baby gift he gave us—it was a custom-made sterling silver rattle in the shape of an anchor."

"Let's go to a room that still has a working computer system," Matt interrupted the flow of reminiscence. "Leif has worked up a file that I think you should see."

After a brief explanation as to who Marcus Kovacs was, and why he was a factor in James Winters's life, Matt ran Leif Anderson's dog-and-pony show. At first Winters shook his head, unbelieving. But as Leif continued fighting for his case, Winters's face subtly changed. By the time the file finished its run, the tough-minded Net Force agent that Matt knew well was looking out of James Winters's eyes.

"This theory of Leif's is by no means conclusive," Captain Winters said. "It could be wishful thinking. On the other hand, it's the first explanation I've heard that works for this nightmare I've been living. And I've been racking my brains for any reason that made sense."

With spare, determined movements, Winters retrieved the datascrip from its system port. Then he engaged the holophone to call the offices of Mitchell, Liddy, and Laird. Stewart Laird was still at work.

"Stay there," Winters crisply told his lawyer. "We're going to reroute the cab you sent to bring Matt here. I want to show you something the Net Force Explorers have uncovered."

"What?" Stewart Laird asked, staring. Obviously, he was

unable to believe the sudden change that had come over his client.

"Better you see it in person rather than over a phone line," Winters replied.

Matt could see a darker, more tactical reason for a personal visit. Whoever had set Winters up for a murder charge would surely have a tap installed on his victim's phone.

Winters smiled at the expression on his lawyer's face. "And cheer up! I was going to contest the cab fare you spent sending Matt to come and see me. This way it becomes a legitimate business expense."

16

Matt could see that the waiting driver was surprised to see two people coming out to his car. He was more surprised—and somewhat dubious—when James Winters told him about the change in destination.

"We're going to the offices of Mitchell, Liddy, and Laird," the captain announced. When he saw the look on the driver's face, he said, "Check with your dispatchers. And have them check with Mr. Laird."

Even when the okay came through, the driver kept shooting his two passengers quizzical looks in the rearview mirror. It couldn't be the change in destination—that wasn't that unusual. No, it was probably that the driver felt he knew Winters's face from somewhere, thanks to all the news coverage. Or perhaps he even recognized the captain. But if so, he didn't say anything. Nobody spoke. Matt was so glad to see Winters shake off that frighteningly lackadaisical attitude he'd shown during their visit—and so shocked by what the captain had told him—that he really couldn't think of anything else to say. As for Winters, the captain seemed downright impatient to get to his lawyer and discuss a defense.

From the continuing looks in the mirror, Matt suspected that the driver really had finally identified Winters as the unwilling star of so many recent news items. The driver's silence was one of suspicion, although that turned to a broad smile when the captain gave him a fat tip on their arrival at the downtown offices of Mitchell, Liddy, and Laird.

Matt and Winters strode through an impressive lobby and rode up in an elevator. All along the way the captain held Leif Anderson's datascrip, tapping it repeatedly with his forefinger.

Steward Laird must have been just as eager. He almost flew into the reception area when they were announced and all but hustled them into his private office. "What have you got?" the lawyer demanded.

"Some information—and a possible description—of someone with the motive and means to create the mess I'm in," Winters replied crisply. "And we have this young man and several of his associates to thank for it."

He took Laird through the original Alcista case—not mentioning why Cynthia Winters was using the car—and the aftermath, explaining how his partner had fabricated evidence to put Alcista away—and how Winters had found out and blown the whistle.

"I'm aware of that much," Laird said. "Michael Steele was cashiered and died soon afterward."

"Perhaps," Winters corrected. "Take a look at this presentation and tell me what you think."

After seeing Leif's show-and-tell and hearing how I-on Investigations made its amazing profits, Laird got on the phone. "We keep a private investigator on retainer—a somewhat more ethical investigator than the ones I just heard about. I want him to see this and start looking into Marcus Kovacs. This isn't enough to convince a jury on its own, but it certainly strikes me as a fruitful line for investigation."

The lawyer's conversation with the private eye was brief and to the point, requesting a detailed background check on Marcus Kovacs and I-on Investigations.

Winters interrupted. "You don't know how secure this line is," he said, putting a hand over the holo pickup. "I suggest you don't transmit the datafile electronically or put the file on any networked computer. Use a dedicated machine only. Make a copy of the finished file and have it hand-delivered."

Laird looked incredulous at first. "We have our lines checked—"

"Remember who we're dealing with," Winters warned.

A new expression came over Laird's face as he remembered all the trouble Winters was in. He nodded and completed the call.

"Now that you have an idea who did this to you, does it suggest anything about the way it was done?" the lawyer asked.

Captain Winters nodded grimly. "Iron Mike Steele was a specialist agent at Net Force. His job was figuring out how the bad guys got into computers, so he had a lot of knowledge on how to do just about anything to a computer." Then, as he paused, if anything, Winters became more grim. "He also had a knowledge of the Net Force computer system that any outside hacker would envy."

Matt was abruptly reminded of Hangman Hank Steadman's mocking words. "If someone could infiltrate our systems like that, I'd hire them immediately as a specialist agent."

That was precisely Mike Steele's job description. Matt began to feel hopeful. Maybe, just maybe, the seemingly airtight case Internal Affairs had compiled was beginning to spring leaks.

Winters shook his head. "Mike was very good at his job. When it came to cooking evidence, he'd create a sort of baloney sandwich, slipping false data between a few slices of truth. It almost always passed muster."

Matt thought back to the records Mark Gridley had accessed—the story of how Steele had planted the fake evidence on Alcista. The Net Force agent had used what seemed like an innocuous phone call to sneak a program onto the gangster's system. That program had initiated the incriminating calls, then erased the records—but not so well that Net Force techs couldn't find traces of them.

"Before things, um, hit the fan, did you get any strange calls to your office?" he asked Winters.

The captain frowned. "Now that you mention it, I got the king of all wrong numbers a few days before Alcista died. A telemarketing call, trying to sell me a discount casket. I had a job breaking into the salesman's spiel, telling him he'd gotten an office, not a home number—and the offices of Net Force, at that."

"Speaking of breaking in," Matt said, "were you on the line with this guy long enough for a program to be transmitted in the background?"

Winters gave him a sharp look. "Just like Mike did to Steve the Bull." He thought for a second. "Maybe. And if it implanted a program, that would explain a few things. If there was a program resident in the Net Force system, that informant's call I got could have been generated in-house. I took it for granted that it was an outside call, because it came from my informant—or seemed to."

Now Laird nodded. "But if it came to you through the Net Force computer, there would be no trace of the call through phone company records."

"Nor through the agency phone log," Winters went on. "It would just be an internal record." He grimaced. "Knowing Steele, we can probably change that to an erased internal record."

"But would it be lost and gone forever?" Laird asked. "I could get a subpoena to have the system checked."

Winters shook his head. "I think it would be better to present it as an internal security breach. Jay Gridley will have techs going over the system with fine-tooth combs. They'll find anything there is to find."

But the captain sounded doubtful, and Matt could understand why. Mike Steele's infiltrated program would no doubt have erased itself after erasing the record of the phony phone call. And in the weeks since the deed was done, who knows how much data might have been recorded over the circuits where the Trojan Horse program had resided?

Still, it was a possibility—a chance to shake the case that seemed to be winding around the captain like a hungry python.

An incoming call came to Laird's system. He looked surprised when he saw the caller. "That was fast work," he commented. "You must have barely gotten the datafile."

The lawyer's system was a high-priced model that offered privacy of image and sound, even from people sitting in the office's visitors' chairs.

Laird's newfound confidence suddenly seemed dented. "Looks like we hit a snag on the Kovacs-Steele thing. The first thing my investigator did was pull fingerprint files—Steele's from Net Force, and Kovacs's from the local licensing agency. Not only do they not match, there are wild dissimilarities."

Winters wasn't fazed in the least. "Of course not," he said. "Steele was a specialist agent—a master hacker. If he intended to disappear, the first thing he'd go after were his fingerprints. And, regrettably, he had the access and the knowledge to change them—both there and throughout the Federal system."

Matt nodded. "The confusion would start from the Net Force computers, which we already have to regard as compromised."

Laird turned back to his computer's display, which only looked like a gray storm cloud from where Matt was sitting.

"Keep digging," the lawyer ordered.

"And tell them not to call again," Winters said. "We still don't know if the phone line's secure."

If it's not, Kovacs-Steele will already know we're after him, Matt realized. *This could be a problem.*

Stewart Laird passed the message along and cut the connection. His expression was preoccupied, as if he was already moving on to other matters mentally. The prospect of having some sort of case to present—something besides temporary insanity—seemed to fill the lawyer with energy.

"I'd like to call a press conference," Laird said. "Like it

or not, you're being tried in the court of public opinion. It would be nice to point that out—and maybe have these so-called journalists tearing at one another instead of coming after us."

Winters looked doubtful. "If you mention Kovacs, it will just warn him."

"I'll couch it in general terms," Laird promised. "Suppose I attack the reporting on *Once Around the Clock*—I could say it was sloppy, that they didn't check their facts." He thought for a second. "How about this? They broadcast slanderous untruths, untruths which were not researched and developed by the network staff. That should get the other reporters going after HoloNews, and spark an in-house investigation by the network lawyers."

"I think Kovacs would have to be blind not to figure out that we're on to him." Winters sourly tapped the pickup on Laird's office system. "For all we know, he could have been listening in already."

He flashed a grin at Laird's expression. "Yeah, I know, makes me sound paranoid, but then, that's my business." His expression went serious again. "Okay, go for it without mentioning Kovacs. Let's shake the tree and see what falls out. In the meantime, send a copy of the kids' datafile to Net Force. To Jay Gridley, not to Internal Affairs. I don't trust Steadman not to bury it. I'm pretty sure Jay'll at least order a security check on the computers. And maybe, if we're lucky, he'll turn a really big magnifying glass on Marcus Kovacs."

Laird nodded. "The more resources we can call on, the better," he said, then quickly consulted his watch. "Okay. I think I can set things up for a press conference tomorrow morning, before the noon news." The lawyer hesitated for a second. "I don't think you need to be present."

Winters looked like a man who'd just gotten a reprieve from a firing squad. "I'm sure I can trust you to say what needs to be said."

"All right, then," Stewart Laird said with a little nod. "The other side has been slinging mud at us for a while now. It's about time we knocked some of it back on them."

• • •

It had been an unusually tight day at the O'Malley household. Megan's mom and dad were both freelance writers, which meant they generally set their own schedules. But both of them were up against deadlines, working to finish books. Since coming home from school, Megan had been tied to the computer, making up work she'd skimped on while trying to help Captain Winters.

I will not call Matt Hunter, she told herself. The words had run through her head like a mantra while she ground her way through all her reading assignments in world history.

Right now Megan had a greater interest in more current events—as in how Winters's lawyer had reacted to the file Leif had developed. But her parents were really getting on her case about schoolwork. And, to tell the truth, Bradford Academy was a pretty demanding place, academically speaking. It wouldn't do to fall too far behind. She'd even made the ultimate sacrifice, programming the home system to meet all incoming calls for her with a message and record them for later consumption.

Supper was late. Her brother Sean tried to do the cooking and filled the kitchen with a peculiarly acrid smoke. The O'Malleys wound up waiting for takeout while airing the house out.

So, between one thing and another, it wasn't until the late news that Megan had a chance to catch up with the world.

"I think you'll want to see this," her father said, poking his head into her room.

She followed him to the living room, where a model-perfect newscaster looked very serious sitting in front of a logo that said NET FORCE MURDER?

"A surprising counterattack came today from the lawyer defending Net Force Captain James Winters. Attorney Stewart Laird not only insisted on his client's innocence in the alleged bombing murder of organized-crime figure Stefano 'the Bull' Alcista; he also accused the media of inaccuracy and outright misrepresentation in their coverage of the story. Laird took special aim at HoloNews—"

The image shifted to a lean-faced, balding man standing in a heavily paneled room. "The leader in this savage attack of pack journalism has been *Once Around the Clock*. I don't know how a supposedly respectable newsmagazine could air some of the so-called facts they've presented. The information was obviously unchecked, and apparently didn't even originate with anyone on the network."

Megan pumped a fist into the air. "All right!" she cried. Whatever else, Leif's file had apparently pumped some life into the captain's defense.

The lawyer's image faded, to be replaced with another familiar face. Megan found herself looking at the chubby features of Professor Arthur Wellman.

The newscaster's voice-over provided the bridge. "Support for Laird's allegations came from media analyst and publisher Arthur Wellman."

Wellman sat at his cluttered desk, handling an unlit pipe. "It's unfortunate that media transgressions are usually only scrutinized in the light of the most sensational cases. It takes a Net Force scandal to disclose irresponsible, possibly even unethical, reportage. But *The Fifth Estate* will present the proof in a special issue. . . ."

"Why, that pink-faced little weasel!" Megan burst out. "He's using the captain's case to get a little free advertising for his own rag of a magazine!"

"Well, he seems to back up what Captain Winters's lawyer was saying," Mrs. O'Malley observed. She squinted to look at the channel selector. "Judging from the roasting HoloNews is getting, I'd guess this is some other network."

Wellman's face disappeared, replaced by the newscaster. This time a different heading appeared behind her head— a stylized car crashing into the HoloNews logo.

"In any event, proof for these allegation will be harder to come by. In a late-breaking report HoloNews personality Tori Rush of *Once Around the Clock* was struck and killed by a hit-and-run driver less than an hour ago. Reporting live from George Washington University Hospital is Liz Fortrell . . ."

Megan stared, her whole face slack with shock.

17

Groaning in disbelief, Matt squinched his eyes shut and clung to his pillow. The room was dark—he'd arranged the shades with care. It was Saturday. He had no school and no plans except to make up for recent sleepless nights and yesterday's legal excitement with as much sack time as possible.

Before going to bed last night, he'd personally ordered the house system not to extend the phone chimes into his room. If anybody called him, the answering program would cut in and record a message for him. Nobody would be bothered—especially not Matt.

So why—how—was his father looking in the door of the dim room, telling Matt that David Gray was on the line for him?

Groaning again, Matt crawled out of bed and staggered around the room, bringing the lights up, then engaging the computer components back into the home system. The display system flashed a holographic image of David Gray, looking disgustingly clean and chipper for—

Matt checked the time. Humph. Nearly noon.

"You okay?" David asked. "You're not sick or something?"

"Asleep," Matt replied, trying to rub some life back into his face. "Crashed early last night. Cut myself out of the system—"

"That's why I've been trying to get through to you for the last hour!" David said with some annoyance. "I finally called your dad. You must have hit the hay very early last night—before the late news." He hesitated for a moment. "Tori Rush is dead. Hit-and-run."

Matt's blinking eyes shot open. "Say again?" he demanded.

"Tori Rush came down to Washington 'for unknown reasons,' according to HoloNews. I think we can imagine her reasons for visiting. I don't imagine her bosses were very happy with her after that press conference yesterday. Anyway, she was leaving the local HoloNews offices via a back way—trying to avoid reporters eager to ask embarrassing questions about where she got her information. Now we'll never know. She was cutting across E Street and got nailed by a passing car."

"Is this from the local news nets, or have you got a closer source of information?"

David's father was a detective in the D.C. police force, working the homicide beat.

"You can see some of it on the news, but my sources are a bit closer," David admitted, tight-lipped. "Dad's got the basic on-scene coroner's comments, and a bunch of conflicting accounts from eyewitnesses. She was walking, she was running, she got hit by a car, truck, or bus. At least Dad thinks he can rule out murder by UFO."

"Murder." It was an ugly word that seemed to stick in Matt's throat.

David nodded. "Under the circumstances, it seems like a highly fortuitous accident."

"Does that push your father's investigation closer to the red line?"

"Dad takes every case seriously," David replied. "From what he said, he's barely in the opening rounds of this one.

But I have heard a couple of things that I thought should be passed along. Dad talked to a bunch of suits from HoloNews. They were very clear that no corporate money was used to hire 'improper research assistance,' was the way they put it."

"What a big surprise," Matt mumbled. "Would they really know?"

"Dad thinks so. Even a newsdiva can't go throwing big amounts of money around without explaining to the network bean counters where it's going. And a quick look at the late Ms. Rush's finances doesn't show any checks to I-on Investigations."

"Blast!" Matt said with feeling.

"On the other hand, there is a pattern of cash withdrawals in recent months. Big sums of money left Ms. Rush's accounts . . . and every time right before she broke new scandals on *Once Around the Clock*."

Matt scowled. "So now we have some suggestive facts to back up the hearsay account that Tori Rush was paying for information. But we still don't have hard evidence to show who was doing the dirty work, or who was getting the money."

Matt gave David an uneasy glance. "And it looks as though people who know anything about what's going on are beginning to suffer fatal accidents. Should we be doing something about that intern up in New York?"

"Maybe, but I'd call Leif. My dad's a cop down here, not in the NYPD," David pointed out. "Besides, I think our bearded detective friend is trying to save a dam with too many leaks in it. When *The Fifth Estate* comes out with its story, Marcus Kovacs—or whoever—will discover how it feels to have the spotlight of publicity glaring down on him. And there won't be a thing he can do about it."

Megan O'Malley couldn't believe what she was seeing on the evening news. Students gathered outside a shattered building on the Columbia campus while a HoloNews reporter offered the results of instant expertise on the subject of bombs.

"There's no evidence as yet to show if this was the work of terrorists, or some terrible personal act of violence. Shattered windows showered glass on students passing on their way to classes. A research library was destroyed, as well as the offices of Professor Emeritus Arthur Wellman. . . ."

Megan swallowed hard. The outer wall on one of the upper floors had been completely blown out. She thought the room revealed to a light rain looked familiar. The large desk Arthur Wellman had sat behind during their holographic chats was scorched and turned on its side. The camera focused in, climbing up the wrecked building as the reporter went on about rescue efforts and the number of people killed. As the most prominent, Wellman's name led the list.

The holocamera's focus zeroed in on something on the floor by the desk—a briar pipe snapped cleanly in two, the broken wood slick with raindrops. Because this was HoloNews, there was no mention of *The Fifth Estate* or the magazine's connection to the growing Tori Rush scandal.

Megan found herself blinking back tears of pain and anger as she gave the computer orders to find other coverage with the information she sought. It was a fight to control her voice.

The holographic display shifted to one of the other news services, who, behind their shocked comments on the bombing and its effect on the Rush case, seemed downright gleeful.

"The sole set of files for the upcoming issue of Wellman's news review, *The Fifth Estate,* was contained in the late professor's computer system." The thin female news reporter struggled to keep an umbrella over her perfect blond hair as she spoke into a microphone. "Only yesterday, Wellman had announced that his publication was prepared to reveal details of unprofessional conduct by HoloNews anchor Tori Rush. Rush herself perished recently in a suspicious hit-and-run incident, while avoiding reporters' questions on the propriety of her information-gathering methods. She was rumored to be hiring covert operatives for illegal Net taps and surveillance in several high-profile exposés. But this mysterious explosion leaves reporters—and the public at large—without the hard facts to prove or disprove these allegations. And, unless the data can be recovered—a job which will require many experts and perhaps months of time—we may never find out.

"Did Tori Rush's journalistic ambitions drag an entire network into the murky business of creating news? She seems to have taken the ultimate means of avoiding comment. Or was it forced upon her? Live from the Columbia campus, this is Rebecca Rostenkovsky. Now back to you, Arlen."

Rumors, allegations, Megan thought in disgust. *That's sufficient for the easy standards of broadcast journalism. Enough for the viewing audience to swallow. But we may end up with nothing on hand to bring Marcus Kovacs to trial.*

She noticed that none of the news reports about the Rush case had actually mentioned Kovacs by name. *Sure. He's the president of a profitable company with lots of lawyers on retainer. The newspeople are watching their step around him. While a public servant like the captain gets the same sort of treatment a fly gets from a steamroller.*

Megan smeared the tears from her cheeks with the back of her hand. Even if there was enough evidence to bring Kovacs to court, his pet lawyers could probably keep dancing around the issues for months. Certainly long enough to outlast the short attention span of the news. Maybe long enough to let him arrange another escape.

Like Alcista killing the captain's wife, Megan thought. *It's happening all over again.*

A more chilling consideration invaded Megan's thinking. Tori Rush had been found out for her use of detectives, and had died before she could tell the world exactly which detectives she'd used. Arthur Wellman had stuck up his head—and had it blown off.

Who else might be a target from being involved in—or getting involved in—the affairs of Marcus Kovacs? Bodie Fuhrman? Leif? Matt Hunter?

Frowning, Megan switched the systems from entertainment mode to communication. She had a bunch of calls to make.

Matt Hunter walked up the quiet suburban block to James Winters's house. He'd gotten the invitation to come over just after supper—and just after a near-lunatic message from Megan O'Malley.

At least it had seemed crazy at the time. Matt slowed down and really began scanning the street as Megan's warning finally began sinking in. There was no doubt that Kovacs, or Steele, or whatever he was calling himself, was a cold-blooded character who didn't hesitate to commit murder or create convenient "accidents."

Matt suddenly had the image of ringing Winters's doorbell and having the whole place blow up. He could almost see the headlines: STUDENT DIES IN MENTOR'S BOMB SUICIDE.

Who could necessarily prove that the bomb hadn't been planted if that happened?

He stood for a long moment in front of the door before finally hitting the doorbell button. Even then, Matt couldn't help blinking his eyes shut.

The door opened, and he found himself standing in front of Captain Winters. "Something blow into your eye, Matt?"

Embarrassed, Matt blinked a couple more times. "Yeah," he lied. "But I think it's out now." He turned inquiring eyes to the captain.

"I'm glad you could come over." Winters led the way to the living room. "Talking with you the other day seemed to help clear the fog out from between my ears." The captain grinned back over his shoulder. "I'm hoping the same thing will happen this evening." Winters indicated a seat on the sofa. "Sorry to drag you out here again. But until this is over, I can't expect any Net links to be secure—up to and including connections to Net Force itself." He hesitated. "Can I get you anything? A soda?"

Matt declined the offer, looking a little confused at the spectacle of James Winters edging around a subject.

Captain Winters sat down. "I wanted to talk to someone

about the new twists in the case, and realized I didn't have a wide range of people to choose from. My military friends only know what they hear on the news shows. And as for my Net Force associates, they're tied up in other ways."

So he's turning to a high-school kid to act as a sounding board, Matt thought. *I don't know if that's funny or sad.*

"I'll try to do my best, Captain," he promised.

"So far, that's been pretty good," Winters said. "I've been banging heads with my lawyer since Tori Rush died, over whether to mention the name Marcus Kovacs in our press conferences, even though we don't have proof of what he's been up to—or who he is. Laird wants to build a case before making accusations. He feels it will make us more credible with the media."

"And you?" Matt asked.

"Full speed ahead, and damn the torpedoes!" Winters admitted. "Shine a spotlight on Kovacs, and it will be difficult for him to do anything." The captain grimaced. "Believe me, I know. I've lived through it."

"I don't know," Matt said. "There was a lot of light shining around Tori Rush. And around Professor Wellman, if it comes to that. That didn't stop what happened to them."

Winters's expression grew more grim. "We're getting stuck in a losing game. Laird doesn't want me to name Kovacs until we have proof. But Kovacs is eliminating anyone who can prove what he was doing."

"Too bad we don't have a solid piece of evidence, instead of people's say-so," Matt said.

Winters stared at the young Explorer. "A solid piece of evidence," he repeated. "Something to prove that Kovacs has something he wants kept secret. Something that proves he's actually Mike Steele!"

The captain bounded to his feet. "Excuse me a moment," he said, crossing the room to a wall unit across from the picture window. Winters knelt, pulling open one of the drawers in the big wooden unit's base.

Even from where he was sitting, Matt caught a faint musty smell. It was as if those drawers hadn't been opened in—how long?

Winters gently searched through the contents of the drawer, shook his head, and closed up the unit again. He moved to the other side, to another drawer. Carefully he ran a hand along the rear of the drawer, rummaging for something.

"Got it!" he exclaimed, pushing the drawer shut and rising to his feet.

Dangling from his hand on a set of drawstrings was a suede pouch.

Captain Winters had an odd expression on his face as he returned to the couch. "Mike Steele was a confirmed bachelor," he said, almost affectionately. "This was his idea of how to wrap a present. He took it out of the jeweler's box and left it in the pouch. Luckily, it has the name of the jeweler on it."

"I don't think—" Matt began.

"This is the baby present Mike gave us." With careful motions, Winters undid the knot in the drawstrings and pulled the bag open. A silver object in the shape of a ship's anchor gleamed in the bottom of the bag.

"It's one of a kind, ridiculously expensive. But Mike was a bachelor, and he loved boats." Winters's mood of gentle reminiscence faded. "This time it may sink him, though. The piece can be traced. The store where he got this still exists, and they'll have records."

"I still don't—" Matt began.

Winters cut him off. "Fingerprints! I know how jewelers work. They shine up any piece before the customer gets it. At most, I expect there are four sets of prints on this thing. Mine, my wife's, the jeweler's sales clerk . . . and Mike Steele's."

"After four years?" Matt asked in disbelief.

"The rattle has sat undisturbed all that time," Winters replied. "We tucked it in the back of a drawer—" He took a deep breath. "I haven't looked at it since. But it kept well. No tarnish. And the FBI has the technology to bring up prints that have sat around on objects much longer. We may only be lucky enough to get a partial fingerprint. A baby rattle isn't the biggest thing in the world, and we probably smudged each others' prints looking at it."

His eyes burned into Matt's. "But even with a partial print from this, I bet we'll be able to find a match with Marcus Kovacs's prints on file for his investigator's license."

Winters smiled a deadly smile. "And why would our Hungarian friend be handling a supposedly dead Net Force agent's baby gift?"

18

Leif Anderson shot a suspicious glance right and left along the block as he stepped out of the expensive apartment building he called home. Like most New Yorkers, he'd normally have thought nothing about darting across the street in the middle of the block if it saved him a couple of steps on the way to the deli where he could satisfy his craving for mint-chocolate ice cream.

That was before Megan's warning call, however. Now, whenever he left the house, Leif found himself slightly on edge about being attacked by a hit-and-run driver.

One day, he thought, *I'm going to end up choking that girl. If I live that long.*

His attention was so concentrated on the traffic, he almost missed the figure darting toward him from the darkened service entrance of a nearby building. Leif just caught a suggestion of motion at the corner of his vision.

His Net Force self-defense training kicked in, however. And, given the strained condition of his nerves, it wasn't exactly surprising that he went with the old saying "The best defense is a strong offense."

Leif swung around, throwing a punch—

And realized his "attacker" was Bodie Fuhrman.

She flinched away so violently, she almost fell to the sidewalk, even though he pulled back on his blow.

"What are you doing?" Bodie squeaked.

"I should be asking you that," Leif responded, staring at the girl. Quite frankly, Bodie looked like hell. Her usually wild red curls were matted down on one side, her clothes were dirty. . . . She looked as though she hadn't seen a mirror—or a bed—in a couple of days.

Suddenly self-conscious, Bodie brushed at her grungy clothing. "I haven't been back to the dorm," she said tightly. "A friend of mine up in Westchester had me over for the weekend. Then I heard what happened to Professor Wellman, and when I checked out my answering system, there were these scary messages. . . ."

Leif rolled his eyes. "Megan O'Malley!" He really was going to shoot her one of these days!

"The kid from Washington? Frack that!" Bodie said. "It was all the hang-up calls. Somebody was trying to figure out whether I was in the dorm or not!"

Her green eyes shone with terror. "They must have found out that I was helping with the article for *The Fifth Estate*. Now they're trying to shut me up—just like the professor and Tori. You've got to help me!"

"Me?" Leif repeated in surprise.

"Yes, you, Mr. Pickup Artist." Bodie looked torn between anger and fear, but fear won out. "That girl, Meg. She—"

"Megan," Leif corrected.

"Whoever," Bodie said irritably. "She let it out that you were both Net Force Explorers, trying to help that Winters guy. I got hold of Alexis De Courcy, and he told me you weren't actually Leif Magnuson, but Leif Anderson."

Oh, yes, she was definitely steamed over Leif's little bit of undercover work. But apparently she was willing to overlook that right now.

"Hey, I've been living in the streets for a day now, trying to find you! You have an in with Net Force. You've got to help me!"

Bodie glanced around the almost empty street. "I figured they'd have given you a bodyguard or something."

"That's because I'm not as important as you'll probably be."

Sighing, Leif took Bodie's arm and escorted her into his building. *My parents are just going to love this,* he thought. *Maybe we can get Anna Westering on the case. . . .*

Jay Gridley opened the door to his home and welcomed Matt Hunter. "I've just been hearing from Captain Winters what you and the other Net Force Explorers had been doing for him," the head of Net Force told him. "I don't know that I like all the methods, but I am impressed with your initiative and your results. You certainly managed to run a couple of circles around my I.A. people."

"Internal Affairs has the job of finding people guilty," Matt said. "We had an incentive to do just the opposite."

He followed his host into the house, through the living room, and down the hall to the room that served the combined purposes of home office and Jay Gridley's den. As they came down the hall, Mark Gridley peered out from the doorway of his room, eyes full of curiosity—and a little alarm, Matt noted.

"Sorry, Mark," Jay Gridley told the Squirt. "This has to be a private discussion."

Those few words just about tripled Mark's nervousness. *He thinks his dad is going to hear about him hacking into the Net Force files!* Matt realized. Both he and James Winters had agreed it wouldn't be necessary to reveal that part of the Net Force Explorers' investigation. But there was no way to tell Mark that—not with his father standing right beside Matt.

Trying to ignore the frightened eyes on him, Matt stepped into the den. It was a small room with bookshelves, comfortable chairs, and a set of techno-toys that would set any computer-literate kid drooling. Nowadays, most home computing system components were built to be unobtrusive. You saw the display—either a hologram projector or screen, and maybe a keyboard. Jay Gridley's computer had its guts spread across a large wooden table. That's because some of the components were black-box specials, samples of technology that had yet to find their way into the consumer market.

Matt was so busy trying to identify any new bells and whistles on the system that he didn't notice James Winters until the captain rose from his seat.

Matt's cheeks burned as he shook hands. Jay Gridley had said he'd been speaking with the captain. It just hadn't penetrated Matt's thick skull as to where and when they'd been doing that.

Oddly, Matt saw that the head of Net Force looked just about as ill at ease as Matt felt.

"I owe you a large apology, James," Gridley finally burst out. "It's bad enough you were treated so shamefully, but worse when I think that I was part of it. When this thing with Alcista started, I should have told HoloNews, Tori Rush, and Hank Steadman to take a flying leap."

"Sure," Winters said dryly. "It would only mean trashing the public's perception of Net Force, damaging our relations with the congressmen who control our budget appropriations, and possibly putting your control of the agency at risk."

"I run a high-profile agency. Supposedly I'm a powerful man, or so I keep hearing in the media." Gridley sighed. "I feel as though I turned my back on you."

"You handled a difficult situation in the way your staff suggested," Winters said steadily. "I can't say it was fun, but if it had happened to someone else, I'd probably have advised you to deal with it the same way—to express measured support, and then step back and see where events took the situation."

"I have to say, I'm happier about where events seem to be heading now," Gridley admitted, "at least as far as you are concerned. These murders worry me. . . ."

"That makes two of us," Winters said. "And we're not out of the woods yet. I won't be until we can confirm that Marcus Kovacs is actually Mike Steele, and that he had a motive for the Alcista bombing and everything that happened around it. It would be nice if we can pin him to these recent killings."

He sighed. "And even if we can, there are going to be newspeople ready to charge us with a cover-up."

Gridley looked grim. "The cover-up happened four years ago, when we didn't go public with Steele's evidence tampering and the reason for Alcista's plea bargain."

"Sealed court records." Winters shrugged. "It was part of the deal."

"A deal accepted on the advice of my staff, to keep Net Force from taking a publicity black eye." Gridley rested one arm against a bookcase. "Looking back on it now, we buried a dirty little secret—and it grew up to be a big dirty tree."

"More like 'the weed of crime,' " Winters suggested.

"I'll be glad when the whole blasted thing is pulled up by the roots," Jay Gridley said. "We seem to be getting there. The fingerprint lab has promised to give me the full results of their work by tomorrow. And even if we can't directly link Kovacs and Steele, that college girl up in New York—"

"Bodie Fuhrman," Matt put in.

Gridley nodded. "Nice name. Anyway, she's talking her head off to the NYPD and to our local agents up there. We'll have ample grounds to question Mr. Kovacs about his investigatory efforts for Tori Rush—and his involvement in the demise of Ms. Rush and Professor Wellman."

The head of Net Force looked grim. "We're going to take full jurisdiction in this matter. It's not just the Alcista thing and the destruction of *The Fifth Estate*'s owner and offices. We're dealing with one of our own here."

Both Winters and Matt nodded in silence.

It will really be over once Net Force gets on the job, Matt thought. *When they start pulling at any and every loose string, I suspect the connections between the so-called Marcus Kovacs and all the killings will unravel pretty darned quick.*

"If all goes well, we should be ready to move by tomorrow afternoon," Jay Gridley said briskly. He turned to

Matt. "Until the results actually hit the media, however, I have to ask you to keep things quiet."

"Do we expect any more fireworks from Mike-Marc?" Winters looked a little ill, in spite of the deliberately restrained language he used for murder. "I think he . . . overreacted . . . when he saw his frame job about to crack."

"I just don't want any premature warnings stampeding him into a quick exit," Gridley said somberly. "Mike Steele is not going to come back and haunt us another time." Again, he looked at Matt. "Okay?"

"Got it, sir," Matt said. The mood in the small room seemed to have mellowed now. Both men seemed comfortable in each other's company. Matt figured it was time for him to butt out.

"I guess I'll be heading home," he said.

Jay Gridley nodded, a wry smile on his face. "I'm sure that as soon as you're out of this door, you'll face a barrage of questions as intense as any HoloNews interview. Remember what you just said. No one—not even Mark—is to know what's going down tomorrow."

"You can count on me," Matt said. "Kovacs will get no warning from any Net Force Explorer."

Megan O'Malley sat in front of her computer. She could feel the frown on her face—part of her was not happy with what she was about to do. But she'd made her decision in spite of it.

"Computer," she said. "Net connection. Voice only—no holographic projection. Vocal filter program, mode choice, 'gravel voice.' Route connection through the following nodes . . ."

She then went on to reel off a list of the most heavily trafficked sites on the Net, while throwing in some random-access evasion programs as well. When she finished, it would be the best anti-tracking effort she'd ever come up with.

Megan allowed herself a small smile. At least this was something she could do. The walls of security around I-on Investigations and Marcus Kovacs himself were too powerful to be breached by her hacking. She thought of recruiting the Squirt—he could get her in to cause havoc in Kovacs's home or business system. But she didn't want to drag anyone else in on a personal vendetta.

She didn't know which was worse, seeing a friend and mentor destroyed by a phantom enemy, or knowing who was doing it, and helplessly watch him not only avoid the consequences, but thumb his nose at justice.

But she did know she wasn't putting up with it any longer.

Megan had to do something!

She gave the computer the private communications code for Marcus Kovacs. That had been the one useful item of information she'd been able to dig up in all her hacking. Even with the speed of her computer, there was a bit of a time lag as the signal bounced all over the Net, even popping into sites in other countries.

Ah! There was the *bleep* that meant the connection had been made!

"Hello," a drowsy voice said. Megan had aimed for a time when most normal people would be asleep.

The voice became more alert. "Why isn't there a visual? Is there a problem?"

"I know who you really are." Megan whispered the words, but they were nearly washed out of her own ears by the amplified voice that mimicked her speech. True to its description, it had the hoarse, gravelly tones of an old man.

"Don't be so sure you got yourself off the hook by murdering all those people," she went on. "I think you only postponed the inevitable. But I'm not the patient type. So I took a page from the old Iron Mike Steele playbook. When you don't have evidence to incriminate people, just make it up and plant it on them."

"What—?" Kovacs's voice was sharp now. Obviously, he was fully awake. Best of all, Megan could detect a note of alarm in his voice. Time to wrap this up.

"Search all you like. You'll never know where this little bit of information is hiding. But it will be somewhere, tick,

tick, ticking away, waiting for just the right moment to wreck your life."

She cut the connection and pulled out of the Net, bouncing through another set of cutout addresses to foil any chance of a trace.

The computer finished its program and automatically shut down. Megan flopped back against the cushions of her computer-link couch, feeling drained—and a little silly.

It would be great if she could actually do what she'd threatened. But she didn't know how to pull off such a scam. Not only was it wildly illegal, it was impractical. She hadn't even managed to get access to the guy's computers.

Megan sighed, massaging her temples. But even if what she'd done was little more than an elaborate prank call, Marcus Kovacs—or rather, Mike Steele—knew his number was up. He might get away with taking people's lives, with taking James Winters's reputation, but he knew somebody was on to him.

At least the scuzz-bucket wouldn't get away with his own peace of mind.

19

The next afternoon, after classes, Matt came out the side door of Bradford Academy. He was on his way to the bus, but as he glanced toward the parking lot, he saw a familiar figure.

Captain Winters stood beside what just had to be an unmarked Net Force van. Two agents sat in the front seat of the waiting Dodge SUV.

"Matt!" the captain called. "I thought we'd be able to catch up with you here."

"What's going on, Captain?"

"These gentlemen are just on their way to I-on Investigations to talk to Marcus Kovacs . . . and bring him in."

"So the fingerprint thing turned out okay?"

"Several partial prints were recovered from the silver rattle," Winters confirmed. "Astonishingly, they don't bear any resemblance to the impressions in Mike Steele's files. But they perfectly match segments of Marcus Kovacs's fingerprints on file with the licensing authorities. That's pretty odd, since Mr. Kovacs was still supposedly in the Balkans when I got that piece of silver. There's no record of him ever entering the U.S. until he arrived to take over I-on.

And that baby rattle has never been out of the USA."

Once again Winters looked the very picture of a Net Force agent, every inch the hunter. "Those will be difficult enough questions for him to answer. Adding in what the Fuhrman girl told us about I-on's activities, I think we'll be able to put him through the wringer."

Winters stopped for a second. "Well, not we, exactly. The gentlemen in the car will take care of that. I'm not only too close to the case to handle the investigation, I'm still on suspension."

A cloud seemed to pass over the captain's features, but then he smiled. "On the other hand, Jay Gridley offered you and me the opportunity to ride along—as observers, I guess you'd say. You can't fault the man's sense of justice. Right now neither of us has any police power. But Jay thought we might like to see the payoff on an investigation where we've both made so many contributions . . . and sacrifices."

Gridley certainly got that right, Matt silently agreed.

He glanced at the two athletic-looking men in the van. "And it's all right with them?"

"It's not as though we're going to be in at the kill. We'll just be spectators." Winters pointed to another car parked in the lot. "That's mine," he said. "We'll just follow along, park in some inconspicuous spot, and watch as the so-called Mr. Kovacs is led off. I don't intend to wave or call attention to myself at all. I just want to see this case through. And I thought you might like to join me, as well."

Matt grinned. "How could I say no?" he asked.

The captain introduced him to the two Net Force operatives in the official car, Agents Grandelli and Murray. Grandelli had a face that looked more Irish than Italian, with blunt features and a hint of humor hiding in the quirk of his lips. Murray had a sort of baby face that he tried to counteract with a fierce expression. He looked as though he was working himself up to storm an enemy fortress and kill everybody inside.

They look like typecasting for good cop/bad cop, Matt thought. That was the interrogation technique where one

questioner did his best to terrorize the suspect while the
other tried to soften him with kindness. These two agents
could probably run that exercise in their sleep.

Murray didn't look very welcoming, restraining his
greetings to a nod and a grunt.

Grandelli, however, was more talkative as he shook
hands. He gave Winters a keen glance. "After all this guy
put you through, are you sure you'll be content just to stand
by and watch while he gets his?"

But Winters simply shook his head. "I don't want to do
anything that will allow our friend—or any smart lawyer
he might hire—to squirm out from under the case we've
built. If that means the best I can be is an audience member
for this arrest, so be it. After the events of the last few
weeks, I'll be happy just knowing my old buddy will be
going through the machinery."

"Okay," Grandelli said. "Then let's get this show on the
road."

Winters led Matt over to his car while the Net Force
agents started their engine. By the time he had the car in
gear, they were at the parking lot gate. The captain pulled
in behind them and easily trailed them to the Potomac River
and the bridge to Reston, Virginia.

Reston had enjoyed a building boom about the turn of
the century, and boasted a modest collection of office tow-
ers located at just the right distance from D.C.

I-on Investigations had a floor in a fifteen-story building
quite close to the Newseum, the museum devoted to print
and broadcast media.

I guess that's bizarrely appropriate, Matt thought. *They
were making broadcast history in their own weird sort of
way.*

Taking advantage of their authority, the Net Force operatives pulled in beside a fire hydrant right by the front
door of the building. Matt noticed that Agent Murray took
the precaution of displaying the Net Force seal in the front
windshield.

Nothing more embarrassing than collecting a perp for

questioning downtown and finding your car towed, Matt thought.

Captain Winters had to circle around a bit, finally finding a legal spot across the street. By the time he and Matt were settled, Agents Murray and Grandelli were already inside the building.

Matt noticed that Winters remained slightly crouched behind the wheel of the car, scanning everyone on the street. "Are you expecting trouble?" he asked.

"More like preparing for the unexpected," the captain replied. "The first time I went to nab a corporate big shot in his lair, my partner and I were held up by his receptionist while Mr. Big ran down the stairs."

"So what would you do if you saw Marcus Kovacs running out the door?" Matt asked.

"Stop him," Winters said briefly.

From the way his fingers gripped the wheel of the car, that seemed to translate into "Run him over."

Matt decided this was not the time for idle conversation. They spent several long minutes in silence, until Winters burst out, "What's keeping them?"

That was when Agent Grandelli pushed his way out through the revolving doors . . . alone.

He strode over to the unmarked car, opened the door, and spoke briefly into the microphone hooked under the dashboard. Then his eyes swept the street for a moment, looking for the captain's car. When he spotted Winters, Grandelli hustled across the street.

The captain already had his window down. "Problems?" he asked.

"I'm not sure," Grandelli admitted. "We buzzed right past the firm's receptionist, but Kovacs's secretary told us he'd called in this morning, saying he was taking some personal time. Kovacs's office was empty, and his absence seemed to be for real. The executive staff is running around like proverbial headless chickens. There were supposed to be some big client meetings today, and it was clear they were failing miserably to do things right without the big man in place."

"What now?" Winters asked.

"I left Murray upstairs to make sure no warning calls get out—he's good at that," Grandelli said. "Then I got on the horn to send another team over to Kovacs's home. See if we can catch him there." The agent hesitated for a second. "We didn't see him as a flight risk. He shouldn't have known this was coming."

Matt realized that two sets of eyes were turning on him. "Hey," he said. "Nothing came out of my mouth."

"Yeah," Grandelli said, a little embarrassed. "Well—I'd better get back to the radio."

Matt and the captain sat in silence again. This time it was even more tense than when they'd been waiting to see Kovacs led out.

Pretending to shift in his seat, Matt stole a quick look at his watch. It felt as if sundown should be coming soon. Instead, only a few minutes had passed since Grandelli had spoken to him.

Matt noticed the agent was inside his car, speaking into the microphone again. When Grandelli emerged, he walked slowly across the street, a puzzled frown on his face.

"Mr. K wasn't in his lovely condominium at the Watergate," Grandelli reported. "In fact, nobody seems to have any idea where the heck he might be."

"Hey, folks!" Megan O'Malley called out as she came in the door. "I'm home!"

Since both of her parents worked as freelance writers, she could usually depend on one or both of them to be around when she got back from school. A brother or two might also turn up, back from college classes.

So it was odd when she got no response. It was possible that research of some sort might have sent Mom and Dad venturing out, although the in-house library had an amazing variety of resources. The last time she'd looked, her father was simultaneously researching immigration of the 1890s, the suffragette movement to win votes for women, ghosts, and the Norman invasion of Sicily in the 1080s.

What amazed her was that these were all supposed to tie up in one book.

So nobody was home? The silence was almost eerie.

Still, the situation was a little weird. The weather outside was warm, and the house air conditioners were running full blast. The folks would have turned them down, Megan knew, if they planned going out for any amount of time. Megan decided to check out the kitchen.

"Mom?" she called tentatively. He voice seemed to echo oddly in the air.

"Where'd everybody—" Her sentence broke off in a big gasp when she saw her mother on the floor. Schoolbooks tumbled from Megan's hands and crashed on the floor tiles. She rushed in and dropped to her knees.

Thank God, she's breathing.

No blood, Megan thought. Nor bruises, or any sort of burns or welts. It was almost as if Mom had gently lay down on the floor, curled up, and gone to sleep.

"Mom?" Megan gently shook her. "Hey, Mom!"

Her mother didn't wake up.

Megan's heart was thudding so hard, it was the only thing she could hear. She took a deep breath, forcing herself to be calm as she checked her mother's neck for a pulse. It was there, strong and steady. She needed to call for help.

Acting on a hunch, she popped out of the kitchen, and headed down the hall to the room Dad used as an office. She heard a faint beeping as she came into the room. A second later Megan staggered back, clinging to the door frame. No need to search for her father. He was home, sacked out in his computer chair. Not merely online and virtual, but completely unconscious. The noise she'd heard was a complaint from the machine, because his hands were mashing down on several key computer controls at once.

Megan's heart was hammering away as if she were running the fifty-yard dash, and her breath came in short, shallow gasps. Spinning away from Dad's office, she spotted one of her older brothers in the doorway of his room, on the floor—out cold.

What to do?

Three family members had keeled over. That didn't sound like the result of bad tuna salad. Megan took a step toward the kitchen. Should she start dragging Mom out? Should she go to the living room and call Emergency Services?

No, to both questions, she decided. If this was a gas leak, or carbon monoxide, she was breathing the stuff herself. The thing to do was get out, then call for help.

She dug in her shoulder bag for her wallet-phone even as she dashed into the living room. The floor seemed spongier with every step she took. Either that, or her legs were getting rubbery.

Bad sign, Megan thought. *Means whatever is in here is getting to me as well.*

Her groping fingers encountered her wallet, but seemed to be having a hard time flipping aside her IDs and stuff.

Should still be set to phone mode, Megan thought fuzzily. Who had she called last? Right. Leif. Warned him that what'shisname? might be after them. Silly idea. What was the emergency code?

Inside the bag her fingers didn't seem to belong to her anymore. They fumbled over the foilpack keypad. What should she press? What was she doing here?

That was when she spotted the figure coming toward her. A guy dressed in dark blue slacks and a matching zippered jacket. Could be casual clothes, could be some sort of delivery uniform.

The thing she really noticed was the gas mask covering his face.

Megan knew she only had one chance. She snapped a high kick at the masked intruder. At the same time she stabbed blindly down on the top row of wallet-phone keys.

For about the fifth time in the last few minutes, Megan knew something was wrong. She'd misjudged the distance her kick would have to traverse. Her foot was nowhere near the guy in the gas mask when it was time to recover.

And . . . she couldn't seem to get her balance. She seemed to be flying through the air in slow motion. No, she was falling. No, the room must be turning. Was that the floor or the ceiling coming at her?

She tried to position her arms and body so they would take the force of landing on . . . whatever . . . and turn it into a roll that would bring her back to her feet.

But Megan never felt the impact. She knew her arms were drooping, her head lolling, as if all the bones had been removed from her body.

Strangely, for a brief second, the world seemed to snap into focus.

It's the floor, she thought, seeing the rug at very close quarters.

Then everything went black.

20

Megan didn't know how much time had passed before she regained consciousness. Slowly, though, blackness turned to misty gray, and then she opened her eyes. She found herself in a dimly lit space, on a very narrow, rather hard bed. The wall curved beside her, and the ceiling seemed very close. Megan couldn't go far to explore her new surroundings. One wrist was handcuffed to a railing at the edge of the bed.

The cuffs weren't really necessary. Megan felt as if all the strength had been bled out of her muscles. And the merest motion made her head pound while starting the room spinning sickeningly. Worst of all, the room seemed to move by itself with a horrible slopping sound. Right then the room suddenly heaved up, and so did everything in Megan's stomach.

Now she knew why the basin had been placed beside her pillow. With a supreme effort she forced her body to move, bringing her head over the side of the bunk to barf on the carpeted floor.

Too bad it wasn't expensive carpet. That rebellious thought seemed to help clear Megan's throbbing brain. The floor covering's quality fell somewhere between the stuff found in offices with heavy traffic and Astro-turf.

"That wasn't very friendly." The mild voice coming out of the dimness sounded very disappointed in her.

"Kidnapping didn't seem very friendly to me," Megan replied in a creaky voice. She peered into the semidarkness, finally making out an outline by the wall. Lights came on, and Megan dropped back to the pillow, feeling as if someone were hammering a spike into her head.

"It should pass in a minute," the mild voice assured her.

Megan squinted up. The only guy she could imagine kidnapping her was Marc Kovacs-Mike Steele. But the guy in the gas mask hadn't had Kovacs's big mane of graying black hair. His hair had been cut businessman-short, and it was an unremarkable shade of mousy brown.

Of course, Steele had changed the color and length of his hair to become Kovacs. One thing was sure: Her captor didn't want her to see any alterations he'd made to his face. He was wearing one of those face masks for the worst winter days, with holes for your mouth and eyes, and a sort of beak with a strainer on it for your nose. It was jokingly known as a "mugger's comfort." The thing must be almost unbearably hot in the warm cabin of this boat. . . .

Hey! She'd figured out where she was!

The boat's bobbing on the water—and the smell of the mess she'd made on the carpet—brought another wave of nausea. Megan grit her teeth and moaned.

"I guess you're not a good sailor," her kidnapper said. "Seasick already, and we're not even away from the dock."

"More like aftereffects of that gas you used on me," Megan shot back.

Gas! She suddenly remembered her mother, father, and brother on the floor, out like lights. "What was that stuff you used?" Megan demanded. "My family—"

"Should be fine," her captor assured her. "The gas was designed to creep up on you so you go to sleep. Often people curl up comfortably. You, however, bounced to the floor. I expect you'll have bruises in some unexpected places—not that it will matter to you for very much longer."

He broke off at her glare. "Anyway, I opened the windows to make sure the stuff dissipated," he said gently. "Your folks should wake up with no ill effects."

Except for having their daughter disappear, Megan thought bleakly.

She gave the masked man a hard look. Traces of a brownish mustache could be spotted through the opening in the grate thing at the end of the nose. The man didn't seem to have a beard anymore.

"You presented me with an interesting problem," the man—she decided to call him Mike Steele—said.

"I'm surprised at your subtlety," she shot back. "Usually you seem to blow your problems up."

The masked head nodded. "But in this case, I had to talk to you first. I had to find out what damaging information you'd planted on me, and where."

A little too late, Megan realized that even the best evasive maneuvers of an amateur hacker might not fool an ex–Net Force professional.

Even though she faced death, either from this masked man or from barfing herself inside out, Megan couldn't restrain the harsh laughter that escaped her lips. "There is no incriminating evidence," she gasped. "I saw you getting away with murder, with no one able to stop you. Figured the least I could do was make sure you didn't enjoy it."

"It was a prank call?" Mike Steele sounded very annoyed.

"Yeah. What are you going to do about it? Kill me twice?"

"Believe it or not, I try not to go overboard in the killing department," Steele said. "I did society a favor taking out Steve the Bull. He was a piece of human garbage. Even his former business associates were glad to see him go. Tori Rush had no family. She was a greedy little witch with an inflated sense of her own talent. Everyone she knew, and especially all the people she screamed at—including her agent—won't miss her much."

"And Professor Wellman? Universally respected? Loved by his students?"

"That was a miscalculation," Steele admitted. "He wasn't supposed to be in his office when the bomb went off. But that shouldn't be your concern right now. You must have a bizarre lucky angel sitting on your shoulder. After I, ah, collected you, I got a call from a source of mine in the FBI fingerprint labs. They were going over an oddball item—a baby rattle in the shape of an anchor."

Megan stared. Steele's lips, revealed through the opening in his mask, had twisted in an ironic smile. "It's a present I gave my partner in a former lifetime. Handmade. Unique. Extremely traceable. And even after all these years they lifted some of my prints off it."

"So they *were* on to you all along," Megan growled. "They just didn't tell me!"

"As things turn out, I probably owe you some thanks," Steele said. "If it hadn't been for your call, I'd have been sitting in my office, happy as a clam, when they came to pick me up." His voice lost some of its humor. "Besides, as I said, murder is bad policy, especially if the victim will be missed. Considering what your Net Force Explorer friends did when I framed Jim Winters, I'd hate to see how they'd react if I killed one of you."

Steele's eyes held a strange emotion as he looked down at her. "James always had the knack of bringing out loyalty. Wish he'd just come through in that department for me."

And loyally stood by while you broke the law? Megan asked silently. It didn't seem the thing to say out loud—not when her kidnapper was debating whether she lived or died.

"Anyway, I guess I owe you one," Steele said. "Your tip got me moving just at the right moment. And this time my getaway fund is much fatter."

Megan didn't say anything, but her feelings must have shown on her face.

"As long as you don't see all of my new look—or get the description or name of this boat—I'm not registered as the owner—I think I can let you go." Steele nodded his masked head. "A blindfold, a quiet area of shoreline . . . all we have to do is wait for the tide to turn."

Matt was getting a lift home from Captain Winters when his wallet-phone buzzed in his back pocket. He dug it out, flipped it open, and held it up. "What?" he asked glumly.

"Matt?" Leif Anderson's voice crackled in his ear. "I got a weird call from Megan. Not another 'Beware of Marcus Kovacs.' This was just an open line . . . and a big thump! It got me worried, so I called the O'Malley house. Nobody answered. Not even after several tries."

With both parents working at home and five kids coming in and out, that was definitely unusual. Matt passed the message on to the captain, and got the response he expected. "I'm in the car with Captain Winters. We'll go and check it out right now. Call you back."

The doors of the O'Malley house were locked, but the windows were open—which was odd, since the air conditioners were going. When they heard a low moan coming from the kitchen window, Winters gave Matt a boost inside.

Matt found a green-faced Mrs. O'Malley trying to push herself up off the floor. "Matt? What—" She rubbed a hand across her face. "Was in here cleaning up. Then felt woozy—sleepy."

Matt glanced around. "Did you open the windows?"

Mrs. O'Malley shook her head—then winced.

"So somebody else must have opened them—to clear something out of the house."

He went around to the door and let Captain Winters in. They searched the house, finding Megan's dad and two more O'Malley brothers, recovering from the effects of being sleep-gassed.

"But where's Megan?" Mrs. O'Malley cried. "She should have been home from school—here are her books." She pointed to a set of schoolbooks dumped on the kitchen floor. As the fumes cleared out of her brain, Mrs. O'Malley looked at her rescuers through new eyes. "She's gone, isn't she? That's why you're here."

Captain Winters already had his wallet-phone out, calling

the police and Net Force. Matt could only look at his hands. He'd never felt so helpless in his life.

"Well, now I know how a civilian witness feels," Captain Winters said as he and Matt Hunter resumed their interrupted trip home. As a suspended agent, Winters could take no part in the investigation of Megan O'Malley's kidnapping—except for answering questions.

Both Matt and the captain had had their statements efficiently taken down. Then they'd been politely—but firmly—told to go home.

The thoughts that had been running through Matt's mind, held in check by the presence of Megan's parents, gushed forth as soon as he was alone in the car with Winters.

"It's bad, isn't it?" Matt said. "My folks—Megan's too, I bet—are always saying to me, 'Don't let people take you anywhere, especially if they're up to no good. In private, they can do anything—' " He broke off. "We've got to do something!"

"Knowing Jay Gridley, you can bet he's got every available hand working this case," Winters said. "I was able to schmooze a little bit with the agents who came to talk to the O'Malleys. Net Force is taking Kovacs's office apart bit by bit, looking for evidence of a bolt-hole. The same thing is going on at the swanky condo he's got at the Watergate, and in his summer home in the Blue Ridge country."

The captain shook his head. "I'm surprised at that. The Mike Steele I remember wasn't a mountains kind of guy. He was always off to a beach, on the water. Boats were his thing."

"Yeah," Matt said. "He supposedly died on one. He gave you an anchor rattle as a baby gift."

"Hmmm. So maybe my colleagues are looking in the wrong direction." Winters frowned as he turned the steering wheel. They were less than a block from Matt's house.

"Think your parents would mind if we used your system for a little research?" the captain asked abruptly.

"To help Megan? How could they?"

When they heard what had happened to Megan, Matt's parents were a hundred percent ready to help.

Matt led the way to his room and warmed up his computer system, giving Winters voice access.

"Computer!" the captain snapped. "List, in order of distance from Reston, Virginia, and the Watergate complex, all yacht clubs, marinas, and private docking facilities for small craft."

"Processing," the computer responded.

Matt looked at Winters in surprise. "I thought you'd be going after ship's registries, or whatever you call them."

Captain Winters shook his head. "This is Mike's ace up his sleeve, his line of retreat if everything goes wrong. The country place in the mountains is a very expensive distraction, something to divert the attention of the law from his real getaway route. He won't call attention to his boat by keeping it under his own name."

"Then how are we going to find it?" Matt asked in dismay.

"I'm afraid that will be up to me," Winters replied grimly. "I'll have to go through the names of the boats, one by one, hoping to spot some connection to Steele."

"That's a long shot," Matt couldn't help saying.

Winters nodded. "Which is why I wouldn't even mention it to Net Force. I can't see Jay Gridley disrupting his search pattern in mid-deployment, just on my say-so."

"Information retrieved," the computer announced.

"Let's see just how big a haystack we'll be digging through," the captain said. "Display on visual."

The closest Washington marina was on Buzzard's Point, an area in the throes of redevelopment into a trendy neighborhood. The docks were closed, being rebuilt to service more expensive yachts.

Next closest was a marina south of National Airport. It was located right where the Potomac widened as it approached Chesapeake Bay. Then it seemed that every Virginia town on the coast had boating facilities. And across the bay were more towns in Maryland, not to mention the port cities of Annapolis and Baltimore.

"Small needle, pretty fracking big haystack," Matt mumbled. Louder, he said, "Are you sure there's no way I can help?"

Winters unhappily shook his head. "Since I don't really know what I'm looking for, I don't see how I can teach you to look for it. Steele used to call this part of the job 'playing cowboys and Indians.' It's fishing for the crucial fact among a sea of possibilities, guided by your instinct and experience."

He gave a reminiscent laugh. "Mike loved to mix his metaphors. Cowboys and Indians, all that Viking stuff . . ." He suddenly straightened up. "You know, if you want to give this a try, get a listing of the boats docked at each town on the Virginia shore. Look for Western or Scandinavian connections. I'll do the same across the water. It's a long shot—"

Matt nodded. "But we have to try."

Heading out to the living room, Matt called up his part of the list. He couldn't believe how many vessels were out there—pleasure craft, fishing boats, sailboats . . .

"I feel like I'm getting pretty waterlogged, just sitting here," Matt muttered, unreeling yet another section of the seemingly endless roster of nautical names.

No, this was a particular kind of waterlogged feeling. Between his car rides and computer work, he hadn't seen the inside of a bathroom since before he'd left school. His back teeth were practically floating.

Returning back down the hall, much relieved, Matt paused to stick his head into his own room. Maybe Captain Winters could go for a drink or something. Matt felt pretty thirsty, all of a sudden.

He blinked. A list of names hung in the air in holographic projection. But the captain was nowhere to be seen. Had he been struck with the urge, too? Maybe he was a step before Matt and had gone to the kitchen for something to drink.

But when Matt checked, the captain wasn't in the spare bathroom or in the kitchen.

He seemed to be . . . gone.

Baffled, Matt dashed back to the system in his room. Yes, there was the list of boats. It was some marina in Annapolis—apparently Winters had decided to check the big cities first.

Could he—?

Matt ran an eye down the displayed listing. He stopped beside the entry for a fair-sized cabin cruiser. . . .

The good ship *Skraelling*.

21

Considering the circumstances, Matt wasn't surprised that he wasn't able to get hold of Jay Gridley. The head of Net Force was directing an all-out effort to find Megan O'Malley.

Matt should probably feel glad he'd managed to contact the Net Force Explorers' liaison, Agent Len Dorpff. That, however, had been the easy part of the job. Now he faced the uphill task of convincing Dorpff to believe in Captain Winters's theory—and getting him to act on it.

Dorpff frowned in the display over Matt's computer. "So, you're saying that Marcus Kovacs's home in the Blue Ride—and the preparations for an extended stay in the mountains—these are a blind of some sort?"

Matt nodded eagerly. "He wants us to put our resources and attention there while he makes his escape by boat. That's how Mike Steele got away the last time. He even faked his death in a boating accident. Look at the baby gift he had made for Captain Winters—a rattle in the shape of an anchor. The guy is obviously crazy over boats." He extended his hands toward the image. "It's not my idea. Captain Winters figured it out, and he probably knows Steele better than anybody in Net Force. The captain may even have found the boat and gone there on his own to stop the getaway."

"Yeah. Can you explain this sudden inspiration to me again?"

"We were checking the names of boats, looking for certain connections. It seems that Steele saw law enforcement as a sort of grown-up game of cowboys and Indians. He was also into the mystique of the Vikings. The boat he disappeared on was called the *Knorr*. That's the Scandinavian name for a Viking long ship."

"I'm with you so far," Dorpff said. "So what about this new discovery?"

"I came in to my room to find Winters gone and the list of ships scrolled to a listing for a big cabin cruiser called the *Skraelling*." Matt took a deep breath. "In the old Viking sagas there are stories of captains who sailed to what we now know is North America. They had fights with the people who lived there, whom they called *skraellings*. We'd call them Native Americans—or Indians."

Would Dorpff see the connection? "Mike Steele thought of his Net Force job as cowboys and Indians," Matt said. "So if he went over to the other side—"

"He'd become an Indian—or in Viking-talk, a *skraelling*. Is that where you're going with this?" A frown of indecision twisted Dorpff's thin face. "Interesting. But you're hanging a lot on a single word."

"A single very uncommon word, attached to a powerful boat, close but not too close to Washington, that would serve as a perfect getaway vehicle."

"I'll pass it up the line," Dorpff said. From the sound of his voice, he was impressed but still dubious about the Winters-Hunter theory.

"I expect this is the last thing you'll want to hear," Matt said, "but I've got to say it. When you took over the liaison job, you said you hoped you'd do as well as Captain Winters. Well, one thing he always did was go the extra mile for any of his Net Force Explorers. If Captain Winters had heard this from one of us, and thought it might possibly help save Megan, he'd take it right to the top."

Len Dorpff stared at him for a moment, speechless.

Guess I pushed it too hard, Matt thought.

But then the young agent slowly nodded his head. "You're right, you know," Dorpff said. "When I took this job, that put the Net Force Explorers under my care. I can't hold back when one of my people is in trouble."

He grinned out of the display at Matt and gave him a sketchy salute. "I'll give it my best shot, Matt," he promised. "My best."

Megan had recovered enough from the effects of the gassing that she could sit on the bunk. She couldn't go much farther with her wrist handcuffed to the rail. Mike Steele had been surprisingly good-natured. He'd cleaned up the mess her outraged stomach had made on the carpet and then disappeared.

They still hadn't left the dock. Apparently, there was quite a bit of work to do before the boat would be ready to set off. Either Steele had been so confident in the success of his deception that he hadn't been maintaining his getaway craft, or he'd been super-careful not to be spotted anywhere near it.

After what seemed like hours the kidnapper returned to the cabin. "We should be leaving shortly," he announced. "It should look like someone getting home from work and going for a brief jaunt to clear away the cobwebs. I've also been checking the charts, trying to find someplace isolated enough that you won't be getting people on my tail too soon, but safe enough that you don't drown in case you're stuck when the tide comes back in."

He hesitated for a moment. "I'm glad you were sensible about the whole screaming thing. There's nobody on the docks, and I didn't want to be forced to gag you while you were still queasy from the gas. Getting sick while you're gagged is no joke."

Megan silently agreed. She'd heard of people drowning in their own vomit when they had no place to spew except down their own lungs.

"So, if you can just remain reasonable a little while more, we can end this with no permanent damage on either side."

Megan still kept silent. That would be her last chance to do anything to try and stop this getaway. Under the circumstances, it might be the last thing she did in her life. Behind that obliging exterior, Mike Steele was a desperate man. If she tried to use her martial arts training against him when he came to undo her handcuffs, he certainly wouldn't hesitate to kill her.

Worse, she only had Steele's word that he was going to beach her someplace desolate. What had the pirates in *Treasure Island* said? "Dead men tell no tales."

That would go twice for a dead female Net Force Explorer. Steele would have a lot less to worry about if he tied her unconscious body to a spare anchor and sent her to the bottom of the bay.

The moment of truth was fast coming up, and Megan still hadn't made up her mind what to do.

"I think there's been enough damage done already, Mike," a new voice cut in.

Both Megan and Steele whirled in surprise to the cabin's entranceway. James Winters stood in the opening, tapping a large wrench into his right hand.

"Threatened with my own wrench," Mike Steele said lightly. "I guess that's the best you could find since they stuck you on the bow-and-arrow squad." Mike glanced at Megan. "That's cop slang—"

"For people who aren't allowed to keep their guns," she finished. "I know."

"No more moving," Winters said. "And keep your hands where I can see them, or I'll brain you where you stand."

He'd picked a good place for this confrontation. The cabin was too cramped for Steele to maneuver, and Steele was close enough to the entrance for Winters to make good on his threat if his ex-partner tried to draw a weapon.

"So what do we do now, Jim?" Steele asked, ostentatiously keeping his hands spread out by his sides. "Stand around and wait till the cavalry comes?"

"As long as you stay on this boat, you'll have the hope

of pulling something off," Winters said. "And, knowing you, you might just succeed."

He tensed, half-raising the wrench. "First, you can give Megan the keys to those cuffs."

"I could just as easily be a gentleman—undo them for her," Steele suggested, his right hand going into his pocket.

"Just the keys," Winters repeated grimly. "If anything else comes out, you'll regret it."

Steele shrugged. "And I thought a few years on a desk might have softened you." Slowly, carefully, his hand emerged, his fingers delicately holding a small ring with a couple of tiny keys on it.

"If you thought I'd have them on the same ring as the ignition for the engines, too bad." The kidnapper grinned. "Of course, if you want to come in and search me for them and any artillery . . ."

Coming into the cramped cabin would bring Winters into hand-to-hand range, and he obviously didn't want to take that chance.

"Toss the keys to Megan," he repeated.

Steele stood with the keys in his palm. "Or what? You'll bash in my skull a couple of times?" He shook his head. "I don't think so, Jim. You'd never do that to an unarmed man."

"People change." Winters's voice sounded like two huge rocks grinding together. "You did. Are you really willing to bet that I haven't?"

Steele silently regarded his ex-partner for a moment. Then, without another word, he tossed the keys to Megan.

It only took a couple of seconds to undo the cuff around her wrist. Another twist of the key, and she removed the jangling bit of metal from around the bed railing.

We may yet need these, she thought.

"Okay, now we're going out on deck," Winters announced. "You'll go first, Mike. Megan, I want you to stay as far as possible from his hands."

Megan nodded. She had no idea how Mike Steele had rated in unarmed combat. But her own martial arts training was chock-full of all sorts of unpleasant holds that could disable an opponent, hold a hostage . . . or break a neck.

Winters waited until Steele was coming toward him before he stepped aside. He stayed at Steele's back as Megan stepped into the open.

Steele spread his arms and took a deep breath. "Ah, that good sea air. It'll be a perfect evening for a sail."

"For other people," Winters said grimly. "Not for you."

"I truly didn't think you'd hold so much of a grudge." Steele almost seemed to be complaining. "You ruined my life, I took a shot at ruining yours. Okay, I lose. But I think you still owe me, Jim. Let me go, and I'm out of your life for good. I swear it. I'll even tell you where you can find the stuff that will clear you completely. All you have to do is stroll onto the dock and let ol' Iron Mike sail away. Come on, Jim. For old times' sake."

"I always wondered if I should have kept quiet when I found that Alcista was framed," James Winters said quietly to his partner's back.

"Things would have been a lot different," Steele said.

"But then I wondered if there were other cases that I just never found out about."

Steele grinned over his shoulder. "I'll never tell."

"But this time around, you went too far. There are three recent cases of murder to consider."

"Two cases are people who are no great loss, and one was an unfortunate accident."

"Three dead people," Winters said. "I can't let you walk away from that." His voice hardened into cop mode. "Onto the dock. Now."

Steele made his move as they were coming down the gangplank. He pushed Megan into James Winters, knocking his former partner off balance. While Winters grabbed Megan to keep her from falling overboard, Iron Mike vaulted over the side and landed on the dock below like a cat, drawing a pistol as he landed.

Megan froze. The gun was trained on her. Its muzzle looked more like a drainage pipe—almost large enough to crawl into.

"I've got her dead in my sights, Jim. Now it's your turn not to do anything stupid."

The wrench dropped from Winters's hand to clatter on the metal gangplank.

"Now, if the two of you will kindly step off and get out of my way . . ."

The distant banshee wail of sirens cut into his words.

"Just get moving," Steele ordered. "I think that's my cue to go."

"Mike, you're not going anywhere," Winters spoke in a rush. "Before I went to the cabin, I was down in the engine room, messing with your fuel pumps. Why do you think I had the wrench with me?"

"You always could think fast," Steele complimented. "And I give you a ten for sincerity. Now do as I say. Get the hell out of my way."

He extended the pistol at arm's length, aiming at Megan.

"All right!" Winters choked. He started down the metal ramp. Megan followed, feeling an invisible target sign burn into her chest.

"Okay," Steele said as they reached the dock. "Let's be traditional about this. Hands up, and stand over there."

His right hand kept the pistol leveled at Megan. His left indicated a position nearly back on land. Besides the sirens, Megan could hear the roar of heavy-duty engines. The cops or Net Force must almost be there.

"Mike, I'm not conning you," Winters insisted as they moved where Steele wanted them. "There's loose fuel in the engine room. Vapors could turn this whole boat into a bomb."

"Just a gamble I'll have to take, pardner." Steele showed remarkable agility as he backed up the gangplank, still keeping them covered.

He just made it aboard as a fleet of cars screeched to a halt at the dock entrance.

"Police! Freeze!" an amplified voice blared as Mike Steele dived into the cockpit. He fired a couple of shots to keep the cops' heads down while he turned the ignition key.

James Winters lunged toward Megan, grabbing her in a

tackle and bringing her to the surface of the dock.

Behind them, a fireball erupted from the bowels of the cabin cruiser. Even lying flat, they could feel the shock wave tear at them. And, at the center of the blast, they heard a terrible human scream.

Flames roared around the superstructure of the vessel as Megan rose to her feet with an assist from James Winters's arm. He tried to draw her along to the dock entrance, where a group of cops and Net Force agents stared at the sudden destruction. But Megan pulled back, her eyes on the worst of the blaze—the cockpit where Mike Steele had stood a moment before.

"He didn't leave you hung out to dry this time," she told her mentor. "I can testify that he confessed to killing those people. And he actually fired shots at the cops trying to stop him. We're all witnesses to that," she finally said. "I mean, there's no misinterpreting that. He didn't succeed, Captain. He's out of your life, and he didn't get you."

James Winters slowly nodded, looking into the flames. "As for the rest . . . well, Iron Mike Steele got the Viking funeral he always wanted. End of story."

Together, they turned away from the blazing wreckage and headed up the dock to dry land.

To safety.